MW01127667

The Glorious Yacht

A New Sherlock Holmes Mystery

Note to Readers:

Your enjoyment of this new Sherlock Holmes mystery will be enhanced by re-reading the original story that inspired this one –

The Gloria Scott.

It has been appended and may be found in the back portion of this book.

The Glorious Yacht

A New Sherlock Holmes
Mystery

Craig Stephen Copland

Published by:

Conservative Growth
1101 30th Street NW. Ste. 500
Washington, DC 20007

Cover design by Rita Toews.

ISBN-13: 978-1539816027

ISBN-10: 1539816028

Dedication

To:

They that go down to the sea in ships, that do business in great waters.

Acknowledgements

Like all writers of Sherlock Holmes fan fiction, I owe a debt to Sir Arthur Conan Doyle. Or, if you are a true Sherlockian, to Dr. John Watson, who recorded the brilliant exploits of the world's most famous detective. This particular novella is a tribute to the original story, *The Gloria Scott*.

In all my stories I drop in unacknowledged quotes and references as tributes to other writers and events. I hope you enjoy spotting them as much as I did inserting them.

A special thanks is given to my dear friend, Mary Engelking, who yet again shared ideas and improvements for the story and encourages me to keep on writing Sherlocks.

Several friends read draft versions of this story and made valuable edits and suggestions, mostly related to sections that needed to be cut. My thanks to all of them. I also acknowledge the dear friends and family who continue to encourage me in this pleasant if quixotic quest of writing a new mystery to correspond to every story in the original Canon.

Contents

Chapter One   The Night of April 15, 1912.................................... 1

Chapter Two   A Morning to Remember 7

Chapter Three   Cowes Week 19

Chapter Four   Recruited to the Indefatigable 25

Chapter Five   The Race to Fastnet 31

Chapter Six   The Night Turns Hostile 37

Chapter Seven   Confined Below the Deck - 45

Chapter Eight   Into the Storm - 53

Chapter Nine   Return to Safe Harbor 61

Chapter Ten   The Past is Prologue 67

Epilogue 71

Historical Notes 73

About the Author 77

More Historical Mysteries by Craig Stephen Copland 79

The Gloria Scott: The Original Sherlock Holmes Mystery 99

Chapter One
The Night of April 15, 1912

"Come my friends," said Sherlock Holmes, " 'tis not too late to seek a newer world. Push off, shall we?"

"My dear Holmes," I said to my old companion, "you tempt us, but it is just not practical. And poetry will not help."

"When was any adventure practical? A year in America would be a splendid experience for you and your wife."

"Please, you and I are both now over sixty years of age and I confess that spending a year in Chicago with you is just too overwhelming a change to consider. I fear I do not have the zeal that I would have had thirty years ago."

"Ah, Watson. Tho' much is taken, much abides; and tho' we are not now that strength which in old days moved earth and heaven, that which we are, we are; One equal temper of heroic hearts, made weak by time and fate, but strong in will to strive, to seek, to find, and not to yield!

"Are you certain," he continued, done with Tennyson, "that I cannot convince you? I am setting aside my little property in Sussex and will be on my way in a month. It will not be the same without you."

"Oh, you go," I said, "and be Ulysses and touch the Happy Isles. Mary and I will keep the home fires burning until you return. You haven't even told us what you will be doing there."

"It is somewhat secretive; an assignment that has been requested from Washington and Whitehall. Some international skullduggery tied to whatever Kaiser Billy is doing in Germany. I fear that is all I can tell you at the moment."

"Oh, Sherlock," said my dear wife, "then you go and have the time of you life. And do remember to write. We shall miss you terribly."

Sherlock Holmes leaned back in his chair. He had been our guest for dinner, as he was at least once a month. On this Saturday evening, the sixteenth of April in the year 1912, he had informed us of his most recent calling, arranged by his brother Mycroft on behalf of the Empire. He was off to America and I would miss him awfully, but my life now was far too settled to consider uprooting it.

So we chatted some more and enjoyed our dessert and tea and reminisced, as we often did, about some of the more unusual cases that we had participated in during the years that were now behind us. My adored wife, Mary, tolerated hearing our stories yet one more time and appeared to love us both all the more every time one of the most foolhardy was repeated. At the end of the evening, after a final cigar and brandy, Holmes took his leave.

"I would greatly wish to say that I will write, but most likely I will not. Writing is your department, my friend. But I shall think of you often."

"As we will of you, my beloved old friend," I replied.

We shook hands affectionately. Mary gave him a lingering hug and he made his way out of our home and into the chilly air of the evening. There had been a frost the night before and my wife chided him about not dressing appropriately. He smiled, pulled his hat down over his ears, and departed.

We retired to our bed, chatted briefly about our unique and much-loved friend, and fell asleep.

At six-thirty the following morning, we were awakened by a loud knocking at the door. It was still dark outside and I pulled on my dressing gown and rushed downstairs, thinking that there must be some sort of medical emergency amongst my patients. I opened the door only to find Sherlock Holmes standing there. He was casually dressed but unshaven and looking distraught.

"Good heavens, Holmes. What is it?"

"I am dreadfully sorry to disturb you, but I am afraid that my emotions, such as they are, have got the better of me. Would you mind terribly if I came in? You are the only true friends I have in London and I felt I had to be with someone on this terrible morning."

"Sherlock," said my wife, who had also donned her dressing gown and come down the stairs. "What is wrong?"

He said nothing but removed his coat and sat down at the table. From his pocket he pulled out the early edition of *The Times* and spread it open. We gasped in horror at the headline.

TITANIC SINKS
OVER 1500 FEARED LOST

"Oh, dear God, no!" cried my wife. "No. It's not possible."

I was speechless, totally stunned by the terrible headline. In silence, the three of us huddled close to each other and read the story. The details were still scarce but reports sent by wireless from ships that rescued the survivors indicated that the worst maritime disaster in history had taken place on the night of 15 April. On its maiden voyage, the "unsinkable" *Titanic* had struck an iceberg off the coast of Newfoundland and had gone to the bottom of the ocean. Over fifteen hundred souls had perished. The reports were still preliminary but there was no doubt that a disaster of unspeakable horror had happened.

Without speaking, Holmes turned the page to the passenger list. The names of those reported to have been rescued were at the top. Those missing and presumed drowned followed. Holmes placed his hand at the top of the latter column and slowly ran it down the list. Many of the names of the first class passengers were familiar. They were names that the general populace recognized from the business and society pages of the press; the great majority of them being those of men. Most of the women and children in first class had been rescued. Several of those who had perished had been clients of Holmes in years past.

We continued through the second class. Every so often I recognized the name of one of my former patients, or of a member of a patient's family. Holmes paused his finger tips many times at names he knew, his encyclopedic memory for people he had met or investigated was now a source of distress, not of utility. As we reached the third class section I could hear my wife starting to sniffle and I turned and noticed tears streaming down her graceful face.

"Dear God," she whispered. "There are so many. So many of them. And the mothers and children are all there too. It's terrible."

When the horrible task of reading through the names was over, my wife put her arms through mine and Holmes's and held us both tightly. We remained that way for some time. Then Holmes reached out his hand to the page in front of us and placed his index finger on a name in the first class list of victims.

"Do you remember Victor?" he asked me. His finger had landed on the name of Victor Emmanuel Trentacost of Donnithorpe, Norfolk.

I thought briefly and yes, I remembered Victor Trentacost. It had been over thirty years, but I remembered him acutely well.

"He was your friend from your college days," I said. "The chap who took us sailing."

"Yes, that was he," said Holmes. "I have had several thousand acquaintances over the years, but other than you, he was the only man I could truly call my friend. And, I must say, that our sailing venture with him was rather memorable."

"What!" exclaimed my wife. "You two? Sailors? That is just too much to believe."

Holmes smiled. "My dear Mrs. Watson, both your husband and I promised Victor we would never speak of it. It would have humiliated him beyond words and destroyed his career. And your astonishment at hearing of our unlikely venture at sea is proof that your stalwart husband kept his word as I did mine."

"John," she said, looking at me with some degree of accusation in her glance. "You never once mentioned this. Come now. Out with it."

I did not answer her directly but turned to Holmes.

"Did Victor have any family?" I asked.

"No. He was an only child. His mother, you may recall, died tragically whilst he was a toddler and, like me, he was a confirmed bachelor. We met once or twice a year at his club for lunch and he assured me that his horses, his tenants, and his constituents were all the family he ever wanted."

"Are we then," I asked, "released from our vow, if he has now gone to his eternal reward?"

Holmes pondered for a moment. "I do suppose we are, and it

5

might take our minds off this terrible tragedy if we could have a morning tea and you tell your dear and long-suffering wife our tale. It would be a fitting eulogy to Victor. He was a generous soul and I am sure he would approve. I assume that you remember it."

"As if it were yesterday," I said. "I distinctly remember that over the course of three days I was swept overboard, nearly drowned, had a pistol jammed against my head, and was knocked silly by a swinging boom. I came closer to death in those three days than in all my time in Afghanistan. So yes, Holmes, thirty years may have passed but I cannot forget a minute of it."

Chapter Two
A Morning to Remember

A nd so it was that the three of us, on that terrible morning in April 1912, attempted to pay our tribute to Victor Trentacost, a true gentleman, and put the tragic news of the day out of our minds for an hour or two.

I recounted the tale of *The Glorious Yacht*.

Later that day, I took pen to paper and put the story on record. What follows are my memories, assisted in places by Holmes's, of what took place thirty-two years ago, in the glorious summer of 1881.

Holmes and I were much younger then, and much poorer. We had met the year before and decided to share lodgings on Baker Street in hopes of stretching our meager incomes. He had achieved some success in solving a handful of cases and I had written the story of one of them, *A Study in Scarlet,* and succeeded in getting it published, but to a disappointing paucity of notice and sales.

In late July of 1881, we both found ourselves with little to do. During the summer months the average Englishman is too concerned with his holiday plans either to take sick or to engage in crime. So it was a welcomed occasion when a note arrived from Holmes's college friend, Victor Trentacost. If my memory serves me correctly, the note ran, more or less:

```
My dear Sherlock:

    I am desperately hoping that this note
finds you well but unencumbered. Next week
is Cowes Week along the Solent and my
irascible father has insisted on my joining
him there whilst he and his equally
insufferable friends race their cutter in
the annual regattas. I cannot abide such
frivolity and the prospect of a week in
their company appalls me. If it is at all
possible, could you and John Watson come and
join me? I will joyfully cover all of your
expenses if you will only agree to offer
conversation beyond the endless repeating of
tales of the sea. Awaiting your reply, with
earnest hope,

    Your friend,

    Victor
```

Holmes and I looked at each other, shrugged our shoulders, and in unison said, "Why not?"

The Solent is the channel of water on England's south coast that separates the Isle of Wight from the mainland. The town of Cowes occupies the northern tip of the island, and across the channel and somewhat to the east sits the city of Portsmouth. In the Solent, being sheltered from the ocean, the waves are not overly large but the currents and tides can be treacherous due to the intersecting of the flow from the Southampton waters and the powerful currents of the great open expanse of the English Channel.

Every year, for several decades now, a week of regattas and festivities, Cowes Week, has been held in the town and on the mainland. Hundreds of boats of all classes come and race, and parties continue well into the night. The culmination of the week is a magnificent display of fireworks. I had only been to sea two times in my life, those being my journeys from England to India and back again when I served in the fighting in Afghanistan. My voyage out was pleasant and hopeful. The return voyage, aboard the *Orentes*, was a dreadful experience that I have tried unsuccessfully to forget. Any prospect of spending time on board a ship again was distinctly unappealing. The opportunity, however, of a midsummer week during which I remained firmly on shore, watching the colorful races whilst sipping chilled gin and engaging in pleasant banter was most attractive.

I confess that I was rather thrilled with that prospect.

Victor met us at Portsmouth Station on Sunday afternoon, 31 July. He was an exceptionally striking young man whose tall, thin body towered over me and even somewhat over Holmes. He had a fair and flawless complexion and a full head of wavy blond hair.

He was beaming from ear to ear.

"Thank you, Sherlock. Thank you, John. You cannot imagine how grateful I am that you agreed to come. The thought of a week in the company of my father and his raucous friends was giving me perfectly awful fits of angst."

"Oh, Victor," said Holmes. "Your dear father is not such a bad chap. I met him whilst we are at college. He is jovial and dotes on you terribly."

"Oh, I know, he loves me dearly and has been mother and father to me for my entire life. When we are alone we get along famously. But when his four friends join him they become entirely unbearable. They drink copious amounts of rum and tell the same stories of their adventures at sea over and over again. Some of them are inexcusably lewd and lead me to blush. They flirt shamelessly with barmaids and sing songs that should never be permitted in decent society."

"They sound like a rum lot if ever there was one," said Holmes. "I cannot wait to meet them."

"Oh, you will, soon enough," Victor said.

He hailed a cab for the three of us and we trundled along a few blocks until we reached a small inn in Southsea.

"Father knows the folks who run this place. They are relatives of the Italians he met in Brooklyn. They call it Bush Villas but that, I fear, is only to make it appear to be an English establishment and not run by immigrants from Italy. I do hope you will find it acceptable. We are only here for one night before we cross over to Cowes tomorrow."

"I am sure," I said, "that it will be perfectly acceptable. Is your father here now? I am rather looking forward to meeting him. He strikes me as a somewhat colorful character."

"No. He is in one of his favorite haunts about a mile from here. The good citizens of Portsmouth recently opened a Sailors' Home, something of a club for men from the navy or merchant marine who are stranded between ships. The founders hoped it would be a mission for seamen and contribute to the improvement of their immortal souls, but the sailors soon disabused them of that fallacy."

"Might we," asked Holmes, "walk over and join him there?"

"Really?" said Victor. "Most certainly we could, if you are sure you want to."

"I have found," said Holmes, "that the men of the sea offer a vast depository of insights into the human condition."

"If by 'human condition,'" replied Victor, shaking his head, "you mean the depraved mind, then I agree entirely."

We chuckled as we departed from the cab and entered a substantial house on Elm Grove. As soon as we had crossed the threshold, any doubt of the national origins of the proprietors vanished as we were welcomed by the pleasant odor of garlic and other spices. I began to look forward to dinner.

After leaving our valises in our individual rooms at the inn, we strolled the mile or so to the docks and found the recently opened Sailors' Home. It was an attractive but not ornate red brick building situated two blocks back from the water. The air inside was thick with tobacco smoke and the spacious bar was crowded with men who all looked as if they had spent their lives at sea. Many of them sported full beards and mustaches that did not quite succeed in obscuring their missing and misshapen teeth.

I was somewhat surprised to hear foreign tongues and one or two obviously American accents, and asked concerning same.

"They welcome all sailors here," said Victor, in response to my question. "It matters not what flag you come in under, all are accommodated. But come, let us find my father and hope that he will not do anything to embarrass us whilst we are here."

We shuffled and excused our way through the patrons of the bar and over to the seating area.

"There is my father," said Victor, nodding to a table by the far wall. "In a place like this, he prefers that I address him as Captain, rather than father. I do so to humor him. It keeps the peace."

"We shall do likewise," said Holmes. "He is looking a few years older than I remember, but then so are all of us."

Sitting against the wall, under a large portrait of Sir Francis Drake, was a man whose age I would have placed at around sixty. His hair was still full and dark, with some streaks of white just above his ears. He had heavy eyebrows and something of a Mediterranean look to his countenance. On his head he had a captain's cap, complete with the appropriate gold braid on the brim. In the few moments we stood looking at him, three other men came over, held pieces of paper in front of him to sign, shook his hand, and moved away.

"Is he signing up a crew?" I asked.

"No," replied Victor. "He has already hired three local boys to help him and his friends on the boat. He is recording bets on the schooner race."

As soon as he saw us, Victor's father waved away the other men who were standing in line to talk to him and rose to his feet.

"Ciao! My son, and Signore Sherlock. Wonderful to see you again. Please, please have a seat. Let me order you something to drink. The vino here, as it is all over England, is not fit for monkeys. But they do brew a good beer. And the food is fit only for cattle compared to what they serve on the Continent.

"A round for my son and his friends!" he shouted to the barmaid.

"Forgive me," he said, smiling, "but I lived with Italians for too many years in Brooklyn and I was spoiled with Chianti and prosciutto. But enough of my complaints, you must tell me what you have been doing since I saw your last, Master Holmes."

Holmes, who was not particularly accustomed to speaking about himself, quickly shifted the conversation to the publication of his monograph on tobacco and to observing that the various brands and countries of origin could be identified not only by their ash, but also by their peculiar aromas. Already, he had noted some sixteen varieties here at the sailors' home.

The Captain chatted amiably for a few more minutes and then graciously excused himself so that he could return to the business he was conducting.

The three of us had had enough of suffocating in the smoke-filled interior of the building and pushed and bumped our way out on to the patio. We struck up several conversations with some of the fellows outside but once they learned that we were neither sailors nor gamblers, their interest in us quickly faded.

Taking our leave, we walked down to the water and then along the quays, past the old harbor, and then all the way down the esplanade to the Southsea Castle, before returning to the Bush Terrace for supper. I had assumed that the Captain would be joining us but he did not appear and I thought I heard him finally return sometime close to midnight after the three of us had gone to bed.

The next day, we walked to the docks and boarded a coaster ferry that took us from Portsmouth across the Solent to Cowes. Victor led us to an elegant inn that looked out over the water and I stood on the porch briefly before entering, enjoying the sunshine and the sea breeze, thinking that this had to be one of the finest places on God's good green earth. I rather felt that I was truly a fortunate man to be here and enjoying it.

There was a bit of a queue at the registration desk. In front of us were three quite impressive chaps that I remembered seeing the day before at the Sailors' Home. I overheard them speaking to the innkeeper and their speech immediately betrayed them to be Americans. I pointed to them in silence and gave a questioning look to Victor. He leaned in close to my ear and whispered.

"There are at least a hundred Yanks here for the regatta. It is quite the rivalry. The fight over the America's Cup has become a replay of the American Rebellion and it has spread now to the Cowes races. But all in good sport. And father says that some of them are jolly good sailors and even better gamblers. He says that he and his pals sailed many races against them in Boston and New York years ago and they could always be counted on for a wager of a hundred dollars."

When it came our turn to check in, Holmes, Victor, and I were assigned a large room on the third floor, with a delightful balcony looking out over the sea.

"I do hope you do not object to our all bunking in together," said Victor, somewhat apologetically. "Rooms in the town are scarce as hen's teeth, so we will have to share. I promise not to snore, but if you hear me crying out in my sleep, just ignore me. Just another nightmare. I seem to be prone to them."

Holmes and I assured him that we could be counted on to ignore him completely.

Tea, we were told, would be served at four o'clock and Victor gave us due warning that his father and friends would all be there, so be prepared to be appalled.

"Gentlemen," said Victor as the three of us approached the end of the parlor where a group of men were sitting, "Allow me to introduce my friends. Sherlock Holmes was a classmate of mine whilst we were in college. And this is his friend, Dr. John Watson."

Victor's father stood to greet us. He was a full head shorter than his son and considerably stouter, but in his captain's cap and finely tailored jacket he looked as if he was used to commanding respect.

"Ah, delighted to see you again today, Sherlock. And you too, Doctor. Wonderful that you could come and join us for the week. As a group of old navy men, we are having a round of rum together. What may we offer you? Something to help you relax so that by tomorrow you will have given leave to your common sense and joined us on our boat?"

"Oh, really, father," said Victor on our behalf. "They are here as my guards to make sure that you do not shanghai *me* onto your boat."

The fellows laughed and we sat down to join the merry lot of them. They all appeared to be around sixty years of age and in rude good health. Some might have profited by losing a pound or two, but none was overweight and all were casually but not cheaply dressed.

"This fine gentleman beside you," began Victor's father, "is Senator Thomas Madison. Originally from Bedford. Elected to the legislature in the golden state of California many years ago, and now back in his home and native land where he belongs. And the one beside him is the Reverend John Wesley Jefferson, at one time of the Methodist Church of Virginia. A fine circuit preacher if ever there was one. You know those chaps, don't you? They all rode in circles, thinking they were big wheels, but were usually well-spoken."

The men laughed at this old saw and raised their glasses to the clergyman in their midst.

"If the reflection off the dome of Sir Monroe Quincy is blinding you, we can always draw the shades," he continued, pointing to a large man with a thick torso and a gleaming bald head.

"And that long, skinny drink of water on the end is Dr. Jackson Harrison. But don't ask him to cure whatever ails you, he's a doctor of philosophy who taught at Princeton until he saw the light and made his fortune along with the rest of us in the great American West."

He asked us to introduce ourselves further and I complied, noting my military service and current occupation as a general practitioner. Holmes announced that he had recently established himself as a consulting detective. This elicited claps and chortles of approval.

"Oh no," cried the Senator. "There goes our chance to bribe every judge on the course. Now what are we going to do?" Again, there were guffaws and laughs and some absurd suggested alternatives.

A young barmaid approached the sitting area and asked the group of us to place our order.

"And what's your name, my dear pretty one," asked Sir Monroe.

"Molly, sir," she said, with a bright smile. "My family name is Snow and I am known around here as Miss Molly and I do not mind if you wish to call me that. Everyone else does."

She could not have been more than sixteen years of age, and was a mere slip of a young thing, but seemed quite sure of herself. As she turned around to leave us Sir Monroe gave her a firm slap on her backside. "Oh my, but God was good to you. Would you not agree, Reverend?" he said.

The young woman gave him a sharp look and continued on her way to the kitchen. She returned a few minutes later with a tray of pints of ale, glasses of rum, and a couple of chilled gin and tonics. She graciously distributed all of them until she had only a pint of ale left on the tray. She turned to Sir Monroe, who had ordered the pint, and began to walk toward him when she suddenly stumbled, sending the entire pint sloshing into the chap's startled face.

"Oh, I am so sorry, sir," she said, looking him directly in the eye. "But aren't you glad it wasn't a pot of hot tea?" She then walked on past him, leaving the empty glass in his lap.

It dawned on all of us at the same time that what had happened was no accident and there was a round of applause, even from Sir Monroe.

"Captain," he said, turning to Victor's father, "if I were you I would get my son to marry that girl tomorrow. She's going to give some young man the ride of his life."

The conversation continued amidst laughter as another round of drinks was served and sandwiches were consumed. When the tea was over, Holmes, Victor, and I excused ourselves and gathered out on the porch.

"Quite the merry band," I said. "How in the world did they end up together?"

"At the Royal Navy recruiting station," said Victor. "I believe it was in 1841. They all served on the same ship and have stayed friends for forty years. After they sailed around the world and had done their term, they agreed that America was the land of opportunity and off they went. Every one of them did wonderfully well and made a small fortune. And, being sailors, they would meet every summer in New York or Boston and take part in the boat races. My father was the most knowledgeable yachtsman, so that's why they call him Captain. *Sir* Monroe is most certainly not a knight here in England. He did some service and made generous donations to the Order of St. John, and they made him a Knight of Malta. Senator Tom was elected in California and served two terms. Doc Jackson managed to get himself enrolled in college and I'm told he taught at Princeton, but he does not act in the least like an egghead. But Reverend John Wesley is indeed a rather sober fellow and I've never yet seen him touch a drop of strong drink."

"Where are their wives?" asked Holmes.

"They are all bachelors, claiming that no good woman would ever put up with them, what with their running off with each other to stakes races, and rugby matches, and sailing regattas. My father was married for only a few years when my mum died. He insisted that he was blessed with his first marriage and was satisfied with his joyful memories. So they are all jovial irredeemable bachelors. I would not doubt that they have mistresses aplenty and have sired children in various ports all across the globe, but I am the only offspring that is acknowledged."

Chapter Three
Cowes Week

O n the following morning, the Captain and his mates were on
the water by seven o'clock along with the three local lads they
had hired to crew for them. The gleaming cutter, the *Indefatigable*, was
untied from its mooring and drifted gently away from the shore and
out into the open water. All that the local boys had to do was hold on
to the end of a line as tight or loose as they were told, and not let go.
They did well and would be remunerated handsomely for their
efforts. The large cutter moved gracefully through the waves, the two
foresails and the large mainsail filling out and catching the winds. In
my field glasses I could watch every member, the five older sailors
and the three local lads, all performing their tasks like clockwork.
When they came in for lunch, Holmes greeted them with small flutes
of champagne and proposed a toast. He cheerfully raised a glass to
Dr. Harrison and gave what I assumed was an appropriate Latin toast

of *ire ad infernum,* smiled, and tossed back the drink. The learned doctor also smiled and did likewise.

At one o'clock on the Monday, the regatta was formally begun. There was a full card of races for varying lengths and types of boats. Small open dinghies, sloops, cutters, ketches, and yawls all would compete around several marked courses. Most were triangular but some required the yachts to race all the way down the Solent to the west, pass the Needles beyond the narrow passage at the far end, circle a buoy out in the open channel, and return.

The final race, the finale, would take place on Saturday. It would be the schooner race down the Solent to the east, out into the English Channel, circumnavigating the Isle of Wight, and returning to the finish line from the southeast. Betting on the result had reached a fever pitch.

On the first day, several of the shorter races were held for the small open dinghies, both sloop-rigged and cat-rigged. Some of these were just for the youngsters and we cheered the boys and girls on, all under the age of sixteen, who skillfully tacked and reached and ran free around the triangular course. It was a delight to see a team of a brother and a sister take the first race.

The Indefatigable had an excellent day. It was not the newest boat in the regatta by a long way and those that were newer, sleeker, and lighter had a distinct advantage, but our old sailors knew their stuff and performed well. We cheered them on. At the end of each day they brought the boat back into its mooring buoy and joined us for a pleasant evening.

All was going well, except that every so often I thought that Holmes was acting rather odd. I had no explanation for his behavior, except possibly that he might have been touched by the divine in such a pristine and beautiful natural setting.

He started whistling tunes, something he had never done much of before. I would have brushed it off as behavior inspired by the sublime location except for the fact that all of the tunes he whistled were vaguely familiar to me as hymns that we had sung in chapel when I was a school boy. On the Tuesday it was *Soldiers of Christ, Arise;* on Wednesday he was fixated on *O for a Thousand Tongues to Sing;* and on Thursday he serenaded us with *Love Divine, All Loves Excelling.* By Saturday, the whistling had ceased.

The entire week was idyllic. The weather was sunny, and a light breeze blew constantly. The races were colorful events as were the jugglers, actors, and musicians who performed for us. Several of England's better company bands were present and gave concerts from the band shell. At the close of each day, the crew the Indefatigable rowed in from their boat, slapping each other on the back, and laughing about their accomplishments and failures of the day. I had to note that they appeared to enjoy each other as much as any group of men I had known. That they had been doing so since they first enlisted in the Navy forty years ago was truly admirable.

The afternoon of the Thursday was hot and sultry and upon returning to the dock, two of the chaps, the reverend and the knight, unbuttoned their shirts, tossed them aside, kicked off their shoes, and dived into the refreshing water. I confess that I followed their example and did likewise. They were strong swimmers and I was able to keep myself afloat. After paddling around for at least fifteen minutes we climbed back out feeling utterly refreshed, with our skin and muscles taut and smiles on our faces.

Saturday was the cup race around the Isle of Wight for schooners only. None of our men was participating and we had a delightful day sitting on the lawn by the main dock. At eight o'clock in the morning we watched as forty graceful schooners skillfully crossed the line in a flying start. Their first leg was to east, down the Solent and out into the ocean. The winds were behind them and to the starboard, so the two large sails were let out and the boats sped off. Once they rounded the south corner of the island they would have to come about and then tack their way into the westerlies that blew up the channel. Before long they had passed out of sight but watch-posts had been set up in twenty spots around the circumference of the island, all connected by telegraph, and reports were cabled in to the judges stand. A large board with bold letter cards kept the assembled spectators informed as to which boats were in front and by what margin.

Holmes, Victor, and I did not wander far from the stands, but I was surprised that neither Victor's father nor his pals were with us. From time to time I spotted one or more of them chatting with some of the other boat owners and I assumed, knowing them, that a ripping set of wagers was being placed. However, I also noticed them speaking with some of the regatta officials who, I hoped, were not accepting bribes.

The race took the full day. Cheers went up from the crowd when the reports came in of the first boat to pass Ryde, and then to round Seaview, and then head out into the open Channel. Another cheer came when the first yacht sailed past the great lighthouse at St. Catharine's Point. In the late afternoon, a sign was posted telling us that the leading yacht had arrived at the Needles headland and entered the home stretch back to the finish line. Many spectators who had wandered off during the day now came back and resumed their vantage points close to the shore. Not far from where we now stood were our five old sailors, surrounded by at least twenty other gentlemen who had the look and body contours of the boats' owners.

The hour of seven in the evening had just passed when the first sail was spotted off in the distance to our left. Again a cheer went up and we were on our feet as one by one the beautiful schooners sailed across the finish line, running free with the evening breeze behind them. Soon the prizes would be awarded and the fireworks would begin.

The sun set at a quarter to nine and at least a thousand sailors, owners, and spectators were gathered. Before the first prize was announced, the regatta 'Admiral' called for attention.

"Ladies and gentlemen, sailors all," he shouted. "This has been a glorious week and we have held one of the largest and finest regattas in the history of England."

A cheer went up. He continued.

"Before we hand out all of the prizes, we have a special announcement. It concerns an event that has never before taken place in the history of sailing in Great Britain. There are so many splendid boats and wonderful sailors gathered here, in this one location, that an opportunity has presented itself. A group of boat owners has proposed a truly great sailing race; one that has never happened before. It will be an open race. Any boat may enter. The Black Friars Distillery in Plymouth, the makers of the fine Plymouth Gin, is offering a prize of a thousand pounds. Are you ready to hear what has been proposed?"

Shouts of "aye" and "yes" along with cries of "get on with it" were heard.

"Tomorrow morning all boats are invited to take part in a race down the Solent, through the Needles, down the Channel and out into the Celtic Sea. From there they must sail to the south coast of Ireland and round the Fastnet Rock. The finish line will be in the Plymouth Harbor. Already over one hundred boats have said they will take part. The race around the Fastnet will be one of the greatest sailing races of all time!"

He went on to give further details, but the crowd was all abuzz. Even as the prizes were awarded and the fireworks set off, the talk was all about the Fastnet race, *the great race. The greatest race ever.* It would take most boats almost three days and they would have to pass through some of the most treacherous waters in the nation. Truly, it would be a superb test of sailing prowess.

When we finally returned to the inn, at close to eleven o'clock in the evening, Captain Trentacost and the four old sailors were gathered in the parlor waiting for us. They were all full of the great race and indeed gave themselves some credit for having helped to propose it to the regatta officials. I could see that they were quite serious about the venture, so much so that they were drinking tea instead of rum. They announced that they would soon be off to bed so as to be ready at first light to prepare for the race to Fastnet and back. No doubt many bets had been placed.

Holmes retreated out on to the porch to have a final pipe and look out over the water before retiring. I joined him and enjoyed the sublime view of the moon over the waters. My serenity was interrupted by a cluster of men at the base of the stairs who were chatting, unaware of our presence. I could not hear what they were saying but I recognized them. There were six in total. Three were the local lads who had been hired by our friends to help crew the Indefatigable. The other three were the imposing American chaps that I had stood behind whilst in the registration line earlier in the week. Something about their meeting so late and secretively caused me concern.

"You don't suppose," I said to Holmes, "that those American fellows are trying to poach our local crew? Our men are counting on them for the great race tomorrow. I don't like the look of what's going on."

"Neither do I," said Holmes, "although I doubt whether they are being hired for any other boat."

"Why do you say that?"

"Because those Americans do not have a boat."

He said no more and turned to climb the stairs up to our room, then retired to his bed in silence. I did the same. Victor was already in his bed and fast asleep.

Chapter Four
Recruited to the Indefatigable

At five thirty the following morning, I was awakened by a loud "Wake up lads!" and the turning up of the gaslight. The first glimmer of dawn was slipping in through the windows and my sleepy eyes could make out Captain Trentacost and Sir Monroe standing over us.

"Good heavens, father" said Victor. "What is it?"

"Sorry to do this to you, boys, but something has come up and we need you."

"What's come up?" asked Victor.

"Our local crew has deserted us. They must have been given a better offer. All we got was a note saying that they had fulfilled their obligations to us for the regatta and would not be working for us any longer."

"Well," said Victor. "Where are they? Can you not find them and make them a better offer."

"We can find neither hide nor hair of them. Gone. All three of them."

"What are you going to do?" asked Victor, as if the presence of his father and Sir Munroe waking us up was not an obvious answer.

"We're recruiting the three of you. Now up you get and get dressed, and meet us downstairs for some breakfast before we take you out and show you what you have to do. Hurry. Jump to it."

"Aye, aye, gentlemen," said Holmes, to my surprise. "We shall be as true and loyal as Suleiman was to the Knights. You can count on us."

Holmes's strange behavior never ceased to perplex me. But Victor was having none of it.

"Faaaather," pleaded Victor. "I cannot abide sailing. You know I can't."

"For the next three days, you can learn to abide it," came the reply. "Now get moving or my boot will be up your arse. See you downstairs."

I looked at Holmes and saw that he was already out of his bed and getting dressed.

"Are you honestly going to get on a boat and sail with them?" I asked.

"I suspect that they need us in more ways than they know," he replied and shuffled off out of the room. I shrugged and reminded myself that I was not a bad swimmer and so was not likely to drown. Three days at sea I thought I could manage, and most certainly our men were in a pinch and we were needed.

Whilst I was dressing, Victor came up to me and sat down on my bed.

"Doctor John," he said. "I don't know what to do. It's not just that I do not like sailing. For some reason it terrifies me. The prospect of three days on the ocean frightens me to death but I can't disappoint my father. This race will be the last great hurrah for him and his pals. You wouldn't happen to have anything in your medical bag that I could take? I know there's nothing that can make me brave, but maybe something to render me almost unconscious so I don't have to think."

He looked at me and I could see the desperation in his eyes. I sat down beside him and put my hand on his shoulder.

"The only way," I said, "to get over a paralyzing fear is to conquer it. It's just like falling off a horse. You have to get up and keep going. You can do it."

His lower lip began to tremble. "Oh, please, John. I can't."

I thought for a moment and then came to a solution.

"I have some laudanum. If you take it now you will be floating on a cloud for the next two hours. By that time you'll be on the boat with no way to escape. And then you'll just have to make it through."

I gave him a strong dose and we made our way down for breakfast. I knew that within ten minutes he would be temporarily inhabiting a dream world and was reasonably sure that the joy of being on the ocean on a beautiful morning would help to remove all his fears.

The old sailors were assembled around a table in the breakfast room as I entered.

"Doc," called one of them to me, "can you cook?"

I was not expecting any such question and after recovering my composure, I assured them that I had no such ability whatsoever. I could not recall a single meal in my life that I had cooked for anyone other than myself. I had been provided for by my parents, by school kitchen workers, by the dear ladies at medical school, by the cookies in the army, and most recently, by the blessed Mrs. Hudson. And I was quite certain that Sherlock Holmes's experience was even less than mine.

"We need a cook," stated Captain Trentacost. "One of the local lads was going to do that for us, but he's gone. We'll be out on the water for three days. We have to eat."

In what was either a stroke of fortune or disaster, it so happened that at that moment the young woman, Molly, who had been waiting on us for the past few days, walked into the room to take our breakfast order.

"Miss Molly," said Sir Monroe, "can you cook?"

She gave him quite the look and then replied, "I can cook."

"Have you ever cooked on a boat?" Monroe continued. "Ever worked a galley?"

"I've cooked on a boat," she said.

"Well then," he roared, "will you come and cook for us for the next three days whilst we sail out to Fastnet and back?"

She laughed spontaneously. "You must be daft. Not if you offered me a hundred pounds would I spend three days on a boat with you old bounders."

"You heard what she said," said Monroe. "For two hundred pounds she'll come and cook for us."

Molly looked stunned. Two hundred pounds was more than she would earn in an entire year. She smiled and replied, "It's too early in the morning for your jokes, sir. How do you want your eggs?"

"We're serious, Molly. Two hundred pounds for three days and we promise to behave."

She looked around and gave a glance to each of us. We all smiled and nodded.

"Very well, but if any one of you gets fresh, I'll put poison in your tea."

"Splendid," said the Captain. "as fair a contract as I've ever heard. Would you mind, my dear, being down at the dock in an hour?"

She put down her notepad and departed. The reverend picked it up and continued to take the breakfast order.

An hour later, in the light of early morning, we were all assembled on the Indefatigable. Our motley crew of five old salts, three young landlubbers, and one wisp of a girl slipped away from the mooring and drifted out into the open waters. Victor was smiling dreamily. We had about two hours to learn what we had to know and master our stations. I looked back at the shore, with the morning sun now causing long shadows to fall to the west of the trees and buildings, and thought, for the last time it turned out, that a sailing adventure was a bit of all right.

As I watched, I noticed three men running from the land out on to the pier. Curious, I pulled out my small set of field glasses to look at them. They were the same three American chaps I had observed the previous evening trying to poach away our local boys. Beside me, Sherlock Holmes was observing the same thing.

"Surprised them didn't we." I said. "They probably thought our yacht would be waylaid after they poached our boys. I think we showed them a thing or two. We London landsmen are made of sterner stuff."

Holmes looked at me in friendly condescension. "As you are known to be a gambling man, my dear doctor, I will lay a fiver that those chaps will be waiting for us in Plymouth and could not care a fig about our local crew."

Something was up. I knew Sherlock Holmes all too well to think he would risk five pounds on a bet to which he did not already know the most assured result. I mumbled a decline of his offer.

The Captain gave a quick introduction to terms and tasks. Our boat was quite large for a cutter, nearly seventy feet long. The crew was spread out all along the deck.

"That is not a rope," he said. "It's a line. And those are not piano wires, they're stays. And that thing at the bow is not a pole-sticking-out, it's a bowsprit." And on he went. Victor seemed to be vaguely familiar with everything, gleaned from years of living with his father. Holmes and I were innocents afloat, but, to my surprise, little Miss Molly was fully familiar with everything already. It appeared that she had been on boats many times before.

"My sister and I came fifth in the junior cat-rigged sloops last year," she said. "My father has worked on boats all his life and he taught me."

Our lessons over, I was assigned to the front of the boat or, having been chastised for calling it that, to the *bow*, and given charge of what the Captain called the *Yankee* sail. The Brits, he explained, used another name, but that was what he learned to call it whilst in America. Holmes was given a post at the staysail, not far from my station.

We practiced our roles through the various points of sail. Close, beam, and broad reaches were covered, and then we tacked several times. Unfortunately, explained the skipper, the first leg of the race, west and down the Solent and through the Needle gap, would require us to tack constantly. A cutter was not as agile in coming about as the sloops, but once out on the open water, he assured us, we would make up for lost time.

Chapter Five
The Race to Fastnet

We were as ready as we would ever be and at 8:30 we sailed past the stern of the signal boat and hailed the officials. "Indefatigable, here!" shouted Senator Tom. "Cleared!" came the reply. I looked out over the water and could see at least one hundred boats of all shapes and sizes, each one jockeying to get itself into the best position for the flying start.

At the ten minute mark the first gun sounded and the Captain sailed away from the start line. At five minutes the second gun was fired and we came about a full one hundred and eighty degrees and sailed close to the wind but under controlled speed. At the one minute mark the final warning gun went off and we turned to catch more wind and began to heel over as we raced toward the line. I watched and held my breath as the line approached, knowing that if we crossed before the gun sounded we would have to turn around and do our start all over again. We could not have been more than twenty-five yards from the line and almost on a beam reach when the starter gun went off. We were flying across the waves and near the head of the pack. Several yachts had jumped the gun and had to turn around and repeat the start, but we had done well.

"Good work, there mates!" shouted the skipper. "Now get ready to hike out when the wind picks up. We're going to do a right proud piece of work here." In truth, he peppered his shouts to us with no end of colorful oaths and curses which are best left to your unholy imaginations. The effect, however, of flying over the waves with the wind streaming across my face was intoxicating. I was keeping close eye on Victor to see how he was managing. The laudanum had worn off and I feared his terror of the sea would take over, but he appeared to be caught up in the moment every bit as much as I was. Holmes was uncharacteristically beaming with a smile and actually laughing every time a spray swept across the boat as we plunged down into the trough of the next wave. All across the water of the Solent, I could see sail after sail of sloop, yawl, cutter, ketch, and the occasional schooner. It was one of the most euphoric moments of my life and I was enjoying it to the hilt.

Our first tack had led us toward the north shore of the waterway and we would soon have to come about and take a starboard tack back across.

"Prepare to come about in five minutes," came the command from the Captain.

"No! No!" came a scream from the door of the cabin. Miss Molly was standing there wagging her head from side to side. "Five will take you too close. There's dirty wind off the point. Three minutes, no more!"

It struck me as highly irregular to have a teenaged cook contradicting a sixty-year-old captain, but there she was. The Captain glared at her for several seconds and then shifted his gaze to the fast approaching shore.

"As I said!" he shouted. "Coming about in two minutes!"

He then beckoned with his index finger to Miss Molly and indicated that she was to sit in the seat adjacent to the helm. She came over and sat down.

It took us at least an hour and a dozen more tacks to work our way down the western side of the Solent and then through the gap and around the gleaming white cliffs that towered over the Needles. From there it was smooth sailing on a close reach all the way across the open water and past Swanage. We gave a wide berth to the Swanage Point and I could see the waves crashing and foaming on the rocks and shoals that extended well out into the water. Sailing into a stiff Westerly, we rounded the Durlston headlands and again into the wide open water of the English Channel. We headed on a bearing of 270 degrees and, unless the wind changed, we would just stay the course, passing the Isle of Portland and on to Star Point.

There was now not much to do. So I found myself a cushion and relaxed, enjoying the splendor of the waves and the passing shore. We were all gathered on the deck and the reverend offered an exceptionally well-informed travelogue on the various towns and natural features on the passing shore. Quite the knowledgeable chap.

In the distance I could see the headlands of the Lizard, the southernmost point of Great Britain, and I remembered from my schooldays that we were passing through what was known as *The Graveyard of Ships*. The waters off England's southwest coast were some of the most treacherous on earth. The rocks and shoals that stretched out from the Lizard had claimed many passing boats and countless lives over the past five hundred or more years. I was not worried, however, as I trusted the Captain to swing out into the open waters to the south and give a very wide berth to the dangerous area near the shore.

As we came closer and closer to the Lizard shoals, I started to think that he was cutting it a bit close. Most assuredly we were in a race and shortening the distance by coming as close as possible to sands bars and rocks was an honored strategy, but I kept thinking that he was going to make it a near run thing.

I glanced over at Miss Molly and could see that she was having the same thoughts as I was. When we were no more than one hundred yards from the waves crashing on the rocks, she finally leaped up and shouted at the helmsman.

"Are you daft, man? Get us out away from the shoals before we smash."

He smiled at her. "They're only dangerous if you don't know your way through them. And I'm sure that they have not moved in the past thirty years."

It was now obvious that he was going to run the boat straight through the rocks. I looked around and could see that Holmes and Victor were now standing up and becoming increasingly uncomfortable. What was odd was that the other four men were sitting quietly, smoking nonchalantly, and ignoring the fast-approaching doom of our craft.

"Prepare to come about!" called the Captain.

The old sailors rose and sauntered to their places.

"Ready when you are," shouted the senator.

We were headed directly toward a gap between two massive outcrops of rock that could not have been more that thirty yards apart. I grabbed on to my jib sheet and held my breath, letting it out only after we had sailed smartly between Scylla and Charybdis as if they did not exist. As soon as they were passed, the order was given and we turned a sharp ninety degrees to the south. That was followed by another tack that sent us around an enormous boulder and then back on to our westward course. Twenty minutes and five course changes later, we were back in the open water of the English Channel and aiming for the northern edge of the Scilly Islands.

By the time we sailed past Lion Rock, the sun was low on the western horizon and the gentle constant evening breeze and the night swells had moved across the water. We would cross the Celtic Sea at night, dead reckoning our way to the southern coast of Ireland. By first light we should be somewhere near the Fastnet Rock.

Miss Molly had prepared us an excellent supper and we sat around on the deck entranced by the setting sun, the appearance of Venus, followed by the stars of the summer triangle, and the unmatched sensation of the gentle breath of Zephyr ruffling our hair and caressing our faces.

Dinner done, the bottle of rum came out.

Some men, when they start into their cups become jovial. Some become morose. Others still cease to speak and turn, taciturn, into their hidden inner souls. Sadly, there are a few who get nasty and pugnacious. The senator from California was from the last group. What had started out as an evening of utmost serenity soon gave signs of degenerating into a highly unpleasant conversation. To this day I do not know whom I should still be more angry at; the senator for ruining the atmosphere, or Sherlock Holmes for taking the bait, unable to resist the urge to show off his brilliance.

"So, Sherlock Holmes," began the senator. "I've read some things about you. Quite the egghead, they say."

"I am sure I have been called much worse," Holmes replied.

"They say you can tell all sorts of things about a fellow just by looking at him."

"That has been said."

"Well then, young master Holmes, let's see how smart you really are. How much can you tell me about me? Go ahead. Give it your best try."

"Tom," interrupted Dr. Jackson. "That is really not necessary."

"It is necessary," snapped the senator. "As far as I am concerned this bloke's a charlatan. I'm betting all his so-called brilliance is no more than a few parlor tricks. So, c'mon master Sherlock. Tell me what you know about me. I lay down five pounds that you haven't observed a single thing beyond what you've been told by Victor. Five pounds, master Sherlock. Are you game, or not?"

"Tom," this time said by Reverend John. "That is not a good idea. You're a bit drunk and you know how you get. Let's not do anything you'll regret."

"What?" he shouted back. "Regret losing a fiver? It wouldn't be the first time, but I'm not going to lose. I'm going to win if this Mister Detective has the spine to take me up on my wager."

I was prepared to dig into my pocket and find a five pound note to give to Holmes with the direction that he should just hand it over to the older man, take a loss, and not make a fuss when, to my eternal dismay, Holmes rose, walked over to Senator Tom and laid a note beside his.

"I accept."

Something was telling me that this was not a good idea. Bad things were about to happen.

"Ha!" said the senator, and he tossed back another shot of rum. "A proud young fool about to be parted from his money. I love wagers against fools. So get on with it, young fellow. Tell me my story."

Holmes, in what I can only admit was his insufferable arrogance, leaned back and slowly lit his pipe and gave a long slow puff, before responding.

"You are an imposter."

Chapter Six
The Night Turns Hostile

What had begun as a delightful night on the Celtic Sea immediately changed to one of tension and hostility.

"Am I now?" said the senator. "Those are fighting words, lad, so you better back them up on the double before I come over and punch your lights out."

Holmes took another puff and turned to Victor.

"Victor, tell the senator how old you are."

Victor was at a loss but mumbled, "What? Thirty-two. Why?"

"And how old were you when your father and his friends came back to England from America?"

"Three. But what does that have to do with anything?"

"So that means that all of these chaps have been in England since the year 1852. That is simple arithmetic, is it not?"

No one answered. We were waiting for the other shoe to drop.

"You claim, sir," Holmes said to the senator, "to have served two terms in the state legislature of California. I am sorry to have to inform you that California was not incorporated as a state within the United States of America until 1851. There was no senate prior to that time in which you could have been a senator. Wherever you were doing the years before you came back to England, you were not in Sacramento serving in elected office."

The light had now gone from the sky and all we had to see by was a storm lantern that hung from the boom. But in the faint light I could see an angry cloud covering the face of the senator. Fortunately the reverend intervened.

"Ha! He got you on that one, Tom. You're right, Mister Holmes, Tom was not a true senator. It was more like a councilor in some town along the west coast. But if a man wants a high and mighty title in the classless society of America, then *senator* is as good as it comes. So Tom's our senator, aren't you Tom? C'mon there mate, he got you on that one, so slide over the fiver."

There was a round of claps and ha-ha's directed by the men to the not-quite-senator and he shrugged and handed over his note to the chap next to him so that it could be passed along to Holmes.

Holmes should have stopped there. He did not.

"Thank you, sir," he said to Reverend John. "I would say 'thank you, reverend' except for the fact that you are likewise an imposter and are not nor have ever been a member of the Methodist clergy."

"Really," bellowed Tom, now becoming belligerent. "You're insulting my friend, Holmes. Now you better take back those words and apologize if you know what's good for you."

"What would be good," said Holmes, "is that a Methodist minister would have a least a passing knowledge of the great hymns of his church. On several occasions I have whistled the hymns of Charles Wesley within earshot of our supposed clergyman and there was not the least flash of recognition. You may, sir," he said, now to Mr. John, "have darkened the door of a church from time to time,

38

but you have never been a man of the cloth. And sir, I would wager a fiver on that one."

John Wesley Jefferson leaned back and crossed his arms over his chest and smiled.

"You have me as well, young man. But, I must say, this is getting interesting. Why don't you keep going on the rest of us?"

Holmes took the bait yet again and turned to Dr. Jackson Harrison.

"Sir, you are posing as a learned man, a doctor of philosophy. Yet on Tuesday I raised a toast to you, uttered a well-known Latin phrase, and you responded with a smile and wished me the same."

"I remember so doing."

"What I said to you, sir, might be best translated as 'go to hell' and you were not in the least offended. That would lead me to believe that either you are a most tolerant gentleman with an uncanny knowledge of the coast of southwest England, or that you are someone else entirely and do not know a single word of the classical language."

Without giving the chap a chance to reply, he then turned to Sir Monroe.

"Sir Monroe, when agreeing to come on board this boat I pledged to you the service and loyalty of Suleiman. Anyone who is truly a Knight of Malta knows that Suleiman the Magnificent was not your friend. The Turk was your sworn enemy and almost eliminated your order from the earth during the Great Siege of Malta. And yet you smiled and thanked me."

Finally he turned to the Captain.

"Captain Trentacost, you are the father of my friend and have generously extended your hospitality to me in the past, for which I thank you. I will refrain from any unmasking if you so desire."

"You've come too far, Sherlock," Captain Trentacost replied.

"You may as well keep going. The truth will out soon enough after what you have already said. My son is now a full-grown man and it's about time he learned the truth of his father's early life. So proceed."

Holmes turned to Victor with a questioning look. Victor shrugged his shoulders and nodded.

"May as well."

"Very well, then. Victor informed me that your occasionally odd way of pronouncing your words was a result of your living in Brooklyn whilst serving as a captain in America's merchant marine. That, sir, is not likely the case. Your accent and syntax betray a boyhood spent not in England but in Italy; most likely in Sicily. Unlike your friends, you have not adopted a name composed of one borrowed from American presidents or famous clergy. You have kept your own and anglicized it. *Trentacosta* is a common family name in Sicily. *Trentacost* is not an English name at all and there is no family history of that name in any part of Norfolk. You clearly have excellent navigational skills to the point of expert knowledge of the shoals, reefs, and rocks off of England's coast. I suspect strongly that it is there that you acquired your sailing experience and not on the east coast of America."

Holmes now leaned back, looking quite smug and self-satisfied.

"Do you, Captain, or any of you wish to contradict me? No? I rather thought so. And would you like me to continue?"

Nothing was said. His question met with glares of animosity.

"Very well, then. I will take your silence as consent and continue. It is a common practice amongst navy men to put a tattoo of the first ship on which they served on their upper arms. When you removed your shirts and took a swim I could see that those of you in the water had such tattoos. However, on the underside of all your wrists is a smaller tattoo, again of a ship, a schooner. I had glimpses of this ship on all of you and most clearly whilst you were swimming. The ribbon under the ship reads *Glorious*. According to *Jane's*, there has never been a ship of the line, or a supply ship, or a vessel in the English merchant marine by that name.

"On the other hand, there *was* a schooner called Glorious that sailed off the southwest coast of England during the years of 1840 to 1845. The annals of crime record that it carried out numerous highly successful pirate attacks on merchant boats and private yachts for several years. The press called the villains the *gentlemen pirates* because of their practice of never harming the crews or passengers of the boats they apprehended, or doing any damage to the vessels. Possibly that was a result of the pirates all having soft hearts and the crews' claiming to be orphans, but more likely it was good business practice, knowing that if you were able to capture a boat once, you could capture it again the following year, and there are reports of one boat having been taken three times."

"Four," came the sharp comment from Sir Monroe.

"I stand corrected, sir," said Holmes. "Truly, these pirates were astute businessmen. Unfortunately, Lloyds became tired of paying for the losses and demanded that the Royal Navy put an end to this nonsense. Whereupon, the pirates wisely sailed across the Atlantic and began to ply their trade in the waters off New England and all the way south to Virginia. They became increasingly specialized in their craft. They ignored large American vessels that might have armed militia on board and concentrated on the yachts of the rich and shameless, of whom there are many on the east coast of America. Rich bankers, industrialists, and occasional politicians were kidnapped and held for ransom. They were surprisingly easy targets and the amount demanded for their safe return was always within the reach of their bank accounts. It proved to be highly successful venture and some in the press who covered the crimes claimed that in excess of one million dollars was extracted over a five-year period."

"Nonsense!" snapped Sir Monroe. All heads turned and looked at him. He ran his hand across his bald head and grinned. "It was more than two million." His colleagues chuckled and nodded.

"Again, sir, I stand corrected," said Holmes. "Allow me to continue. In the fall of 1851 there was a hurricane off the Atlantic coast and many ships and lives were lost. The wreck of the Glorious washed up on the Chesapeake shore and it was concluded that all on board had perished at sea. There were, although, persistent rumors that the crew had escaped, and sightings of them were reported first in Ocean City and later in Baltimore. And then all trace of them vanished.

"If my memory serves me correctly," Homes went on, "the names of the gentlemen pirates were ..." Here he paused, closed his eyes and joined his hands in front of his chin, with the fingertips pressed together. "Ah, yes. I believe that they were Samuel White, Henry Longbough, Fredrick Yeats, Hyman Whitley, and Victor Emmanuel Trentacosta. Other than the Captain, I do not know which of you is which, but you might wish to introduce yourselves."

He was positively grinning and turned and faced each of the men in the order that they were seated on the deck. For several minutes there was no reply. We sailed on in silence. Finally, Reverend John spoke.

"Young man," he said, "you are too clever by half for your own good. You have unmasked us and uncovered a secret that we have carefully guarded for three decades. In doing so, you have become a threat to the continued enjoyment of our pleasant lives. When you boarded this boat you did so as our friend. I fear you have now become our enemy and we shall have to decide amongst ourselves what to do with you."

From his pocket he withdrew a revolver and pointed it at Holmes. Sir Munroe and Senator Tom also pulled out guns and waved them in Holmes's direction.

Holmes was unflappable. "Permit me, sir to correct you. I may be your best friend in the world at this moment. Your true enemies will be waiting for you on the dock in Plymouth when you complete the race, ready to arrest you, transport you back to America and send you to one of their federal prisons if not the gallows."

He paused, enjoying the dramatic effect his words had had.

"The careful efforts you claim to have made to keep your secret were not sufficient. You have, in fact, been rather careless. So much so that rumors of your pleasant life here in England have continued to float back to America. Three months ago, as I am sure you are aware, Lloyds and The Hartford combined their forces and issued a reward for information leading to your arrest. Bringing you to justice even after so many years will have a deterrent effect on any who have thoughts of repeating your success. You all now have a price on your heads. You do know that, do you not?"

Heads nodded in silence. Holmes carried on.

"And I also assume that you are familiar with the Pinkerton Detective Agency?"

That question brought attention looks of apprehension.

"The three American gentlemen who were staying at the same inn as we are did not once this past week get on a boat. They were busy all week chatting with people. By Saturday they were watching the group of you very closely. On Saturday evening they met with your local crew and I assure you that it was not to hire them as sailors. I strongly suspect that it was to warn them that on Sunday morning they would be arresting you and impounding this boat and that your crew should best not be anywhere nearby or have any further connection to any of you if they knew what was good for them. What those American chaps did not expect was that you would Shanghai the three of us and push off into the water at such an early hour.

"I will wager any one of you," Holmes now announced, "a fiver each, that those Pinkertons will be standing on the pier in Plymouth, accompanied likely by Scotland Yard, and will escort you to your fate as soon as you step off this boat."

Not one of them took up his offer. After several moments of silence, Senator Tom spoke quietly.

"Mr. Holmes, it would be good if you, the doctor, Victor and

Miss Molly retreated down into the cabin for an hour or so. My friends and I need to have a meeting and I do not think you should be part of it."

The night under the moon and stars, with the warm sea breeze wafting over me was as close to paradise as can be found anywhere in England, and I did not relish the prospect of spending the next hour or several hours cooped up in a stuffy cabin. I was about to voice my objection when Holmes, to my surprise, rose and descended the stairs. Victor followed him and so did the young cook. I was not in a good humor as I joined the three of them.

Chapter Seven
Confined Below the Deck

"Well, Holmes," I said after the cabin door closed behind us. "This is a fine mess you got us in to. If you hadn't been so eager to show off, we might still be out there and no one the wiser."

Holmes was about to reply to my obvious anger when Victor put his hand on Holmes's arm, indicating his request for Holmes to remain silent.

"John," said Victor, "he did it for me."

"What do you mean?" I demanded.

"I have known for many years that there was some dark secret in my father's past. I would have died of shame and humiliation had he been arrested, tried in court and then hanged for his crimes of decades ago. Now he has an opportunity to escape and disappear. I know it seems like an unnecessary display of Sherlock's brilliance, but I assure you, I am humbly grateful."

He then turned to Holmes and quietly said, "Thank you, my friend."

Holmes first smiled at Victor and then turned to me, "My dear doctor, you and Victor are the only true friends I have. I would have done then same if it meant protecting you."

I appreciated his sentiments but was still thoroughly annoyed at the prospect of now having to spend the next day and a half locked up below deck. I harrumphed and stretched out on one of the bunks. The other three followed my example and did the same.

I must have dozed off for several hours, lulled by the gentle rocking of the yacht on the night swells. I was awakened by the jovial shout of loud voice.

"Avast there, me mates! Rise and shine! All hands on deck," shouted the Captain.

Rubbing the sleep from my eyes, I looked through the small porthole window and could glimpse first light in the morning sky. I staggered to my feet and out of the cabin.

"Fastnet Rock will soon be upon us. To your stations," continued the orders.

In the distance I saw the emerging dark mound of Fastnet with the spire of the lighthouse silhouetted against the slowly lightening sky. When I glimpsed over the surrounding waters, I noticed the sails of a score other boats beating their way along the same bearing as we were. Several were well in front of us, and a mass of them were trailing. It had become a very strange adventure, but I permitted myself the comforting thought, that, all told, we were doing not too badly in this race.

Within twenty minutes, the mass of Fastnet Rock was looming off the starboard bow. Following the Captain's commands, we tacked several times as we approached and then swung around it. Standing on the lookout deck of the lighthouse was a race signalman. He waved his flags at us and the Captain signaled back.

Ten minutes later, we had changed course a full one hundred and eighty degrees and were headed back on a southeast bearing and across the Celtic Deep. I relaxed and determined to enjoy this most unusual adventure on the sea.

That was not to be.

"Thank you, mates. Well done. Now, back into the cabin," said the Captain.

That was just a bit too much.

"Look here," I said. "There is no reason we cannot stay on deck. It is not as if we can run away."

On my right ear I felt something cold. I turned my head and found myself peering down the barrel of a revolver.

"The captain said, get back into the cabin," said Senator Tom. "Was there some part of the command you failed to understand, doctor?"

I became an obedient if unwilling sailor and shuffled my way back down the staircase. The door of the cabin was closed behind us and I heard a clunking sound coming from the far side of it. I spun around and attempted to open the door, only to find that while the handle turned the door was fast in place. It had been barred somehow from the other side. We had become captives, imprisoned below deck.

"So," said Miss Moly. "Would you blokes like some breakfast? If those old blighters up there dare ask for anything, I'm declaring a mutiny."

We laughed and cheered her on and soon were enjoying a hearty English breakfast, making fun of our increasingly hungry captors above us. I imagined that they would soon be opening up and demanding their victuals.

They did no such thing. An hour passed, and then another. There was no change in our direction or speed.

"Where are we?" I asked of anyone who might have had a better idea than I did.

"We're moving quickly, at about eight to ten knots an hour," said Molly. "We're on a beam reach and if the prevailing winds stay constant, we won't have to tack until we round Lands End. They won't need us on deck until this evening."

I resigned myself to spending what would have been a splendid day in the sunshine confined to a stuffy cabin and filled the time by writing the story of this adventure in my mind. The morning, mid-day, and the afternoon all passed. We chatted with each other from time to time but for the most part remained silent.

Somewhere close to six in the evening, Victor spoke up.

"They must not be hungry," he said.

"Nor need to use the head," added Miss Molly. "Or else they're fouling the ocean."

We offered a few forced chuckles and returned to the doldrums.

As the sun was setting, I had expected the breeze to die down. Instead it was stiffening and the yacht was heeled over more than it had been all day. Molly walked over to the starboard porthole and peered out.

"Oh, ****," I don't like the looks of what's coming our way."

I got up off of my bunk and took a look. The sky to the south had darkened and the shadows of rain falling in the distance were scattered across the southern horizon.

"We're in for a walloper," said Molly. "They're going to need us on board."

Another half hour passed and the wind was now howling around the cabin. The Captain must have been in a hurry to get to a port and then make a run for it in order to escape the Pinkertons for, as far as

I could tell, he had not let out the mainsail and we were now heeled over at a racing angle.

Miss Molly looked out again from the porthole window.

"They're daft. It all lightning out there and it's coming our way."

She walked over to the door and started banging on it.

"You! Out there! You're in a storm. Don't be daft. Open the door and let us out. We're not going to run away!"

There was no response.

She banged harder and shouted louder, but still received no answer.

"I have not been paying attention," said Holmes, "but I do not recall hearing a sound from up above us for at least the past several hours. Either they are sitting in one place silently or they have abandoned ship."

"Bloody, hell," shouted the girl. "Then break down the door, or this thing's going over and we're going down!"

In turn, Victor, Holmes, and I all tried pounding our shoulders against the door, but the position of the doorway in the cabin made it impossible to take a run at it. Try as we might, it did not budge.

"I fear," said Holmes, "that they have barred it securely on the other side. Equipping it in that manner would come in handy when imprisoning kidnapped victims."

He had no sooner spoken these words that we felt the boat heel over sharply to the port side. For a terrible few seconds I held my breath, certain that we were about to roll over. As we righted ourselves a flash of lightning lit up the porthole and the entire boat shook.

"We must find a way out of here," said Holmes. "Is there any tool we can use to unfasten the door hinges?"

This led to a mad scramble as we looked for anything resembling a screwdriver, but to no avail.

I looked over at the porthole. The window covering it was secured with bolts and butterfly nuts. We might be able to unfasten them but the hole was hardly more than sixteen inches across and there was no way we could squeeze through it.

A quiet voice beside me spoke up. "I can get through there."

"Good heavens, child," I exclaimed. "We're not sending you out there to climb up the side of the cabin in the midst of a storm. You'll be blown away."

"No I won't. I'll tie a line onto me and you can pull me back if you have to. Just loosen the clamps and help me get through."

I looked at the other two men and we shrugged and then nodded. I turned to Molly and was somewhat shocked to see that she had dropped her dress on the floor and was standing in the middle of the cabin in just her corset and underwear, busily fastening a bowline around her slender body.

"You're a doctor, right?" she said, looking at me.

"I am."

"Well then you can put your hand on me arse and hold me in the air whilst I wiggle through."

Holmes had undone the fastenings and removed the window. Quick as a wink, Molly raised her hands above her head and extended them and then her head through the narrow opening. I lifted her lithe body in the air. She could not have weighed more than ninety pounds. With one hand on her spine and the other on her posterior, I lifted and shoved while she wriggled.

We were making good progress when a wave suddenly slammed against the side of the boat. Water rushed past her body and into the cabin. I could hear her choking and sputtering, followed by some rather dreadful curses and oaths that were quite unseemly for a girl of her age. I pushed and she wriggled some more and then I felt her body start to move on its own.

"I've got the edge of the deck!" she shouted.

Soon her legs and feet disappeared through the hole and we moved quickly to fasten the window back in place before another wave poured in.

A minute later we heard metallic sounds against the door of the cabin and it swung open.

"There's no one out here. The dinghy's gone," she yelled. In truth, those were not her exact words. What was actually uttered gave evidence of her having spent far too much of her youth in the company of sailors.

The three of us hastened out of the cabin and up onto the deck. The sky was dark and the wind was screaming like a banshee. Rain was falling sideways but the temperature, thankfully, had not dropped more than a few degrees. Victor immediately let out the main sail and the boat righted itself. Holmes and I did likewise to the Yankee and the foresail. Molly had taken over the helm and once I cleated my line in place I walked back to her."

"Any idea where we are?" I asked.

"Not the foggiest."

We sailed on in the dark for several more minutes and then I felt a small hand clasping on to my arm.

"Doctor John," she whispered. "Can you hear that?"

"What?'

"Listen."

Chapter Eight
Into the Storm

I did and I heard a distinct sound that did not seem to be too far in front of us. I looked at our young helmsman.

"What is it?"

"It's breakers. There's rocks or shoreline or shoals or something directly in front of us."

An extended flash of lightning revealed the disaster we were rushing towards. Molly quickly looked back behind us and to both port and starboard.

"Jesus, Mary and Joseph! We're in the middle of the Lizard shoals." And again she added a few choice words that I have not recorded.

"All of you," she shouted. "Tie a line around your body in case you get washed overboard. We're going over the shoal," she shouted.

"And get out on the rail and hike for all you're worth. I'll tip her up on her side and get the keel as far away from the rocks as I can. Haul your sails in hard when I yell."

We instinctively obeyed, found a line, tied one end around our chests and fastened the other end to the base of the mast. Then we hustled to mid-ship, fastened our feet under the hiking strap, and leaned back. The cutter was on a close reach as we headed toward towards the surf breaking over the shoal. I was not sure what Molly was waiting for but suddenly she screamed at us.

"Now! Haul in! Hike!"

As we pulled tight on the lines and hauled the sails in as far as we could, the boat quickly turned so that it was on a beam reach at right angles to the powerful wind. We heeled over, and then heeled some more, and more yet, until I was sure that we were about to turn turtle. I felt a swell lift the boat and carry us into the shoal. On either side of the boat I saw surf emerging as the base of the large wave was breaking up against the rocks below us.

There was a moment when my heart stopped and the boat shuddered. The keel had struck rock and the entire craft was shaking as we touched one, and then another and then another. But we kept moving. It seemed like and eternity but then the bouncing ceased and we were back in open water.

"Right. Let out," came the command from the helm.

We did and the boat came back to a more or less upright position. Again, I clamped my Yankee sail in place and made my way over to Molly at the helm.

"Fine sailing, Captain."

"We're not through yet."

I looked ahead but in the darkness could see nothing. Then another flash of lightning lit up a wall of rock that appeared to extend several hundred feet to starboard.

"There's dark water on the port side," cried Molly. "We have to jibe. Pull in the sails. Hard! Now, and get ready to duck."

I started to run back to my post. Molly swung the boat to the port and the wind caught the back of the mainsail and whipped it around from one side to the other. I ducked but not fast enough or far enough. The boom crashed against the back of my head and sent me sprawling to the deck.

I think that perhaps I was knocked out for a second or two but quickly came to my senses and felt for the back of my head. I could tell that a goose egg would soon be emerging and I forced myself to count to ten backwards and recite the Lord's Prayer. Good. There was no serious damage and I now moved over to join Holmes and Victor on the port rail.

"There's more rocks ahead," our captain shouted. "But there's open sea to the south. Hold on. We're going directly into the waves."

On the ocean, in the dark, it is difficult to estimate the height of a wave as it approaches you. Perhaps experienced sailors have their ways of doing this task but I did not. I assumed that we would simply be rising and falling as if we were on a carriage and galloping through some rolling terrain. The next thing I knew I was struck by a wall of water and doing backward somersaults with water on all sides of me. I felt my ankles strike the rail and then I was upside down falling headfirst into the ocean. I had enough sense to reach for the line I had attached to my chest and start pulling. My first three pulls encountered no resistance. My line was slack. In a second of passing terror, I thought I had broken free of the mast and was adrift. But then it went taut and I began to pull myself hand over hand up toward the surface. A few seconds later I felt a sharp tug on my line and could feel myself being pulled powerfully forward. My head broke the surface of the water and I gasped for air. In the darkness I could see the form of Holmes standing at the edge of the deck and reeling me in.

When I arrived at the side of the boat two sets of hands reached down and grasped my arms and lifted me back on board.

"Really, my dear doctor," said Holmes. "You already went for a swim on Thursday last. Must you do so again?"

Both of us wanted to spare a moment and have a chuckle together but our young captain again shouted at us.

"Back to your posts. We're not done yet."

And true, we were not. For the next ten minutes we slid up one side of a massive wave, crested, and then sped down the other side into the trough. Once we were well away from the rocks and shoals, we swung to the port.

"Any port in a storm. We can sail direct to Coverjack. It's not far," said Captain Molly.

None of us answered her, having no idea whether Coverjack was a good idea or not.

"But it should be clear all the way now to Plymouth," she said. Then paused, and added,

"Are you up for it? Shall we finish the race?"

We gave her a rousing cheer of "Aye, Captain."

"Right then, mates. You can let the sails out. We should be able to run free from here."

We opened the sails and soon we were racing over the great waves with the wind at our back. It was an exhilarating few hours in the middle of the night. And then it stopped. The storm had blown past us and clear skies were coming up from the south along with the first light. The wind dropped and once again we sailed with a light summer breeze.

I looked out over the open water to see if I could see any other yachts. There were none in front of us, but off to the west I noticed a few near the horizon, the morning sun now lighting up their sails.

"I say, Holmes, it looks as if we might be in the lead."

"A pleasant thought, but highly improbable. There were at least a dozen craft ahead of us as we rounded Fastnet."

We set a bearing of fifty-five degrees and cruised towards the finish line some sixty miles in front of us.

We had been on a dead run for about half an hour when I spotted something far out in the water in front of us.

"Molly," I said. "Is that a rock out there? Or is it a marker? That round white object straight ahead."

She strained her eyes and looked intently for a minute.

"It the hull of a boat. Upside down. One of the yachts has flipped over. If there are any sailors in the water we have to go and rescue them. We're the closest boat. It's the law of the sea."

She had us trim the sails and we slowed down. As we got closer we could see several hands waving at us. We were still moving at a good speed and I feared we would run over top of them with no chance to haul them on board.

"We'll have to sail past and come back," said Molly and that is exactly what we attempted to do. There were six men in the water, all clinging to the keel and rudder of their yacht. We exchanged shouts as we neared them and confirmed that all of them were safe and accounted for. Once well past, we came completely about and sailed toward them, close hauled and sailing as close to the wind as our cutter could manage. Once we were almost on top of them, Molly turned the helm quickly and threw us into irons. Holmes, Victor and I had lines in hand ready to heave to the chaps in the water, but the wind was blowing us away from the swamped boat too quickly.

"We'll have to do it again," said Molly. With that, we turned around and sailed away, turned again and sailed back. This time, however, she went about ten yards past the boat, close to its stern, before taking us into irons. Now we drifted backwards toward the overturned vessel. We would have no trouble getting the men out of the water.

"My dear," I whispered to Molly, "I think you might want to run down into the cabin and pull your clothes back on."

She first looked shocked and let loose with one or two more choice words and then laughed and hopped down the staircase.

One by one we lifted in the soaking wet sailors. The waters of the North Atlantic are never warm, even in the middle of summer, and half of the fellows were shivering. But soon we had blankets wrapped around them and they were thanking us profusely. The entire rescue had taken no more than forty-five minutes, but during that time another six yachts passed us on their way to Plymouth. Each of them signaled asking if we needed help. We signaled back that we were fine and they sailed on.

"Gentlemen," said one of the fellows we had rescued, "I am Jeremy Middleton, Marquess of Elderbury, and captain of the formerly wonderful yacht, the *Luck of the Irish*. I reckoned that we were at least half an hour out in first place. We should have trimmed our sails more in the storm but we were a bit too eager for the prize and over we went. We do thank you for your kind assistance."

He then looked more closely at us.

"There's only three of you? That is amazing. Who is the captain?"

"In the cabin," said Holmes. "Up in a minute."

A minute later, Molly emerged from the cabin, fully clothed and with her hair more or less back in place.

"Captain Jeremy," said Holmes. "Allow me to introduce you to Captain Molly Snow of Cowes. One of the finest ever to sail the seven seas."

Victor and I were trying very hard not to laugh at the look of utter bewilderment on Jeremy Middleton's face. He looked at Molly and then at us but we kept our poker faces and gazed placidly out over the sea.

"I say, Captain Molly," said Holmes. "Will you dead reckon us back to Plymouth? Another three hours, what say?"

"Aye, but back to your stations, sailors. I'm sure that these Irish fellows will give you a hand."

And so they did. We chatted amiably with the members of the other crew. I overheard one of them ask Victor how we had done so well in the race. He shrugged his shoulders and with feigned nonchalance said, "Well, you know, if you sail through the shoals rather than around them you can save a great deal of time."

The other chap looked at him in total disbelief.

"But that's impossible!" he sputtered.

Victor turned his head away ever so slightly and looked up into the clouds. "Oh, not really. Not when you have the captain we have."

I bit my tongue and looked at Holmes. He gave me a smile and a wink.

One of their crew was quite a young lad, no more than twenty by the looks of him. He was tall, athletic, and aristocratically handsome. He managed to find a seat directly behind the helm and was soon chatting to our amazing captain.

Chapter Nine
Return to Safe Harbor

By early afternoon, the lighthouse on the Rame Head, the entrance marker for Plymouth Harbor, had come into sight. We rounded it and headed north to our final destination. As we entered the harbor I saw hundreds of people standing on the piers, all waving ribbons and handkerchiefs and cheering us on. Molly steered us to the mooring buoy, we dropped the sails, and a boat from the harbor staff lashed the Indefatigable securely into place. We descended the rope ladder and were taken over to the pier.

Waiting for us were seven men and not one of them looking at all happy.

"Stop where you are!" commanded the smallest one of them. I recognized him immediately. He was a slight chap with a narrow ferret-like face and beady eyes. He held up a badge.

"Inspector Lestrade, Scotland Yard." Behind him stood three

English constables in uniform and behind them the three Pinkertons I had last seen on the dock at Cowes on Sunday morning.

The Inspector turned to the Pinkertons.

"Are these the men you are after?"

"I beg your pardon," said Jeremy Middleton. "Just what do you think is going on here? My crew and I are all men of noble birth and these fine people and this remarkable young lady are the heroes who have not only rescued us but who have successfully completed the Great Fastnet Race."

There is no creature on earth more capable of righteous indignation than a still damp English lord who has recently come close both to victory and drowning. The inspector backed away. The Pinkertons looked us all over carefully.

"Where did the other ones go?" asked one of them.

"What other ones?" snapped Lord Jeremy.

"The four guys who were on this boat when it left Cowes?"

"Oh, those chaps," said Holmes with an air of practiced indifference. "They complained of being sea-sick, or perhaps it was just sick of the sea, so we let them off back a ways."

"Where?"

"Ireland. Yes, I do believe it was Ireland. You might try going there to look for them."

At this point, the inspector recognized Holmes and sputtered his surprise.

"Sherlock Holmes! What in the name of all that is holy were you doing on that boat?"

"Manning the jib sheet."

With that, Holmes sauntered on past them and we followed Jeremy up to the judges' stand.

"Congratulations Indefatigable!" shouted one of the officials.

"Why, thank you sir," said Victor, nodding humbly. "But all we did was what any yacht is expected to do and we came to the rescue of our fellow sailors. There is no need for congratulations. Any other boat would have done the same thing."

"Good heavens, man," said the official. "We're not congratulating you for helping the other boat. We're congratulating you because you won the race."

"That cannot be," said Victor. "At least a dozen boats passed us before we entered the Sound."

"They passed you, sir, because you had stopped to perform a rescue. They are gentlemen, sir, and they have duly reported your act and confirmed that you would easily have won have you not stopped. Not one of them would dream of claiming a prize that rightfully belongs to you. So, well done. Please give the desk the full names of the crew."

For a moment we stood, speechless. Victor, having been raised to be a gentleman, quickly recovered his composure and answered.

"Mr. Sherlock Holmes of London, Doctor John Watson, also of London. I am Victor Emanuel Trentacost of Donnithorpe, and this is Miss Molly Snow of Cowes."

"I assume that Miss Snow was your cook."

"That is correct."

"And which of you chaps is the captain?"

"Miss Snow is our captain"

I will leave it to the reader's imagination to contemplate the next few minutes whilst each of us, backed up by Jeremy and his crew, swore that Miss Molly Snow was indeed both cook and captain of the victorious yacht. The General Manager of Blackfriars then presented us with our cash prizes and bestowed on each of us a case of Plymouth Gin. When handing Molly her case, he somewhat arrogantly inquired if she was old enough to partake of alcoholic spirits. I did not hear what she said in reply but it evinced a look of utter shock on the face of the manager.

We were feted and praised and treated to a fine dinner. Victor graciously stood in for our captain and agreed to address the assembled crowd. Molly had begged off in desperate fear and trembling at the thought of having to give a speech. Throughout the evening, however, I noticed that she continued to attract the attention of the young man from the rescued boat.

The festivities of the evening having finally ended, we were put up in the select Duke of Cornwall Hotel. The staff took our clothes and promised to have them all laundered and pressed by morning. The four members of our intrepid crew, clad in bathrobes, slouched into easy chairs in our suite. Miss Molly was nearly hidden in the large chair beside me, wrapped in a bathrobe that was clearly many sizes too large for her tiny body.

"You appear, my dear," I said, "to have landed yourself a rather large fish today. Quite a catch, I must say."

She blushed furiously. "Oh, Doctor John. His name is Reginald Barclay and he's asked me to come and visit his family on their estate in Sussex. I'm scared stiff."

"My dear, you will be just fine. Make friends with the butler and the head maid and they'll look after you."

"I'll have to mind my Ps and Qs."

"Molly, if you can just manage to mind your ..." And then I let loose with seven of the most forbidden curse words in the English tongue, none of which are ever uttered in polite society and all of which I had heard slip from her pretty young lips over the past forty-eight hours.

"Oh," she blushed again. "Yes. I must try to do that. Gosh and golly."

The next day we boarded a train to Portsmouth and from there took the ferry back to the inn in Cowes to fetch our belongings. The village, so packed and festive just a few days ago was now nearly empty. The sailboats had all departed and the late afternoon sun shone down on the nearly empty bay.

Holmes and I sat out on the porch enjoying tea, which Miss Molly had graciously brought to us. We exchanged a few pleasantries with her and chatted about our recent adventure.

Victor soon appeared. I looked at him and was immediately concerned. His eyes were reddened, as if he had been crying. In his hands were several sheets of paper and an envelope.

Chapter Ten
The Past is Prologue

"Here. You may as well read this. I've read it. And you may as well keep it too. I don't think I will ever need to read it again."

He deposited the letter on the table in front of us and walked away. Holmes read it and handed each page to me as soon as he had finished. The postmark was stamped CORK, and it read:

My dearest son:

I have long feared that the day would come when my son, whom I have loved more than life, learned about my shameful past and that your ways and mine would have to part. I did not expect it to come so suddenly upon me and I and my partners-in-crime are grudgingly grateful to your friend, Sherlock Holmes, for giving us the warning we needed to escape the gallows.

Lord willing, we will be able to meet again in the not-too-distant future, but perhaps not.

I regret having had to abandon ship but knew that it would be best if you did not know where we launched the dinghy in making our escape. I knew that you, and especially Sherlock Holmes, would realize that there was no one left on deck and be clever enough to send the young cook through the window to open the door and sail to the nearest port.

My motley crew will now escape back to America, or possibly Shanghai, or perhaps Buenos Aires. We planned for this day and have deposits in many banks around the world. You need not be concerned for our material well-being.

You are also well provided for. The title to my property in Norfolk is in your name. The rents will provide a comfortable enough income for a gentleman.

There is something else I must confess to you, Victor.

I am not your father.

I took over the responsibility of caring for you and raising you on what was the worst day of my life. As you now know from your friend, Sherlock, we pirated up and down the east coast of America, boarding yachts and kidnapping wealthy members of the sailing crowd, taking care not to harm them, and quickly collecting the ransom. It all went well until one day when a brave but foolish man fired his revolver directly at us. Instinctively, I fired two shots back in his direction to warm him to stop and surrender. As terrible fate would have it, one of the shots struck him and the other your mother. Both died on the deck in front of their two-year-old son.

I did the only thing I could do before God and my conscience, and took you from the boat and adopted you as my son. We then sunk your family's yacht, a sight you also observed and remembered only in your nightmares. Before doing so, I removed all documents that pertained to your family and the boat. As soon as we returned to Boston, and before your family had been declared missing, I went immediately to your home and robbed it. I took no valuables, only all the documents I could find that identified you. These are all locked away in the safe in my office. The key is taped to the bottom of the center drawer.

Seven years after your family disappeared, you were all declared dead and the ownership of your father's estate and his extensive assets passed to your uncle. He is a very wealthy man but entirely honorable. If you present yourself to him, I am sure that he will not only transfer your inheritance to you but will be joyful beyond words to know that you are alive. Your physical resemblance to your father, his older brother, is exceptional.

I understand and accept that you may wish to vanquish me from your life, knowing what you now know. My prayers will be with you until I die.

Your name is not Victor Emanuel Trentacost. It is Charles Cabot Gardner III.

May God bless you, my son.

[This letter has been kept in the files of Sherlock Holmes, undisturbed for the past thirty years. He retrieved it for me so that it could be included completely and accurately in this account. J.H.W.]

Epilogue

17 April 1912. Ten o'clock in the morning.

Having completed our reminiscences, Holmes, Mary, and I raised a cup of tea to the memory of a thoroughly decent and admirable man, Victor Emmanuel Trentacost, and then retired to the porch and enjoyed what had become a lovely April morning, a sad but, in a way, a *glorious* morning.

"You did," I said, "keep in contact with Victor regularly, did you not?"

"I did," said Holmes.

"Did he ever say anything about our time at sea and the Captain who raised him as a son?"

"Yes, he did, and I have honored his request for secrecy. He kept the name he had grown up with and five years after our race to Fastnet, his father contacted him and they re-established some sort of friendship. He forgave his father and they kept exchanging letters and meeting every few years after that, until the old captain passed away."

"Where did they all go after Fastnet?"

"To New York, where they resumed being pirates."

"I beg your pardon!"

"Legally, of course, which is to say they became bankers. They pooled their funds and opened a private bank. And then they took out large and expensive policies with the insurance companies who had been hunting them down and signed up scores of their wealthy clients for life insurance with those same companies. As you might expect, having become far more valuable alive than dead, the bounty on their heads quietly disappeared."

"Holmes," I said. "At times you can be awfully cynical. There is, however, one more question I simply have to ask."

"Then ask."

"Whatever happened to Molly Snow? Is she running an inn in Cowes and tossing beer all over unruly sailors?"

Holmes smiled. "I believe the person you are referring to is now known as Lady Reginald Barclay and the first woman to serve as a governor of the Royal Thames Yacht Club. She is quite the famous regatta captain, and rather well-known for her scandalous language after several rounds of Plymouth Gin."

Did you enjoy this story? Or were there ways it could have been improved? Please take a minute to help the author write and deliver great mysteries to future readers by leaving a review on the site from which you purchased the book.

Thanks,

CSC

Historical Notes

According to The Canon, as recorded in *His Last Bow,* Sherlock Holmes spent considerable time from 1912 through early 1914 in Chicago and Buffalo, infiltrating a network of German spies. He returned to England prior to the outbreak of The Great War so that he could bring down the espionage efforts of Baron Von Bork.

From 1882 to 1890, Arthur Conan Doyle lived at 1 Bush Villa, Elm Grove, Southsea, Portsmouth, and established his first independent medical practice. It was while living there that Doyle created the character of Sherlock Holmes and wrote the first two stories about our beloved detective. Since, in this story, Holmes and Watson have to travel to Portsmouth, it seemed fitting that they should stay in the same place.

The Sailors' Home described in this story was opened around 1850 and in 1855 received a Royal Charter. It has continued from that time until the present as the Royal Maritime Club. It is now a lovely historical hotel and no longer reserved for sailors.

The Cowes Week regattas date back to 1826 and, except for years during the wars, they have continued to be held annually. To this day, they attract hundreds of boats and thousands of participants and spectators. It is one of the great events of the yachting world.

The Fastnet Race did not actually start until 1925. The course is as described in the story and it is famous for being one of the most demanding and dangerous of the world's great sailing races. The race in this story is a fictional proto-type of the Fastnet.

The south coast of Cornwall is well know as "the graveyard of ships" and the shoals, reefs, sandbars, and currents have claimed many ships and lives over the past eight hundred years.

A "cutter" was a popular design of sailboat in the past and a few are still sailed today. It has a large mainsail and two forward sails, with the "Yankee" sail affixed to a bowsprit, whereas a sloop has only one forward sail or jib. Edits from those readers who know more about sailing than I do are welcomed.

The story is a tribute to *The Gloria Scott*, with a nod to *The Pirates of Penzance*.

About the Author

In May of 2014 the Sherlock Holmes Society of Canada – better known as The Bootmakers (www.torontobootmakers.com) – announced a contest for a new Sherlock Holmes story. Although he had no experience writing fiction, the author submitted a short Sherlock Holmes mystery and was blessed to be declared one of the winners. Thus inspired, he has continued to write new Sherlock Holmes Mysteries since and is on a mission to write a new story as a tribute to each of the sixty stories in the original Canon. He currently writes from Toronto, the Okanagan, Tokyo, and Manhattan.

More Historical Mysteries
by Craig Stephen Copland

www.SherlockHolmesMystery.com

Studying Scarlet. Starlet O'Halloran has arrived in London looking for her long lost husband, Brett. She and Momma come to 221B Baker Street seeking the help of Sherlock Holmes. Three men have already been murdered, garroted, by an evil conspiracy. Unexpected events unfold and together Sherlock Holmes, Dr. Watson, Starlet, Brett, and two new members of the clan have to vanquish a band of murderous anarchists, rescue the King and save the British Empire. This is an unauthorized parody, inspired by Arthur Conan Doyle's *A Study in Scarlet* and Margaret Mitchell's *Gone with the Wind.*

A Case of Identity Theft. It is the fall of 1888 and Jack the Ripper is terrorizing London. The national Rugby Union team has just returned from New Zealand and Australia. A young married couple is found, minus their heads. They were both on the team tour. Another young couple is missing and in peril. Sherlock Holmes, Dr. Watson, the couple's mothers, and Mycroft must join forces to find the murderer before he kills again and makes off with half a million pounds. The novella is inspired by the original story by Arthur Conan Doyle, *A Case of Identity.* It will appeal both to devoted fans of Sherlock Holmes, as well as to those who love the great game of rugby.

The Adventure of the Spectred Bat.

A beautiful young woman, just weeks away from giving birth, arrives at Baker Street in the middle of the night. Her sister was attacked by a bat and died and now it is attacking her. Could it be a vampire sent by the local band of Gypsies? Sherlock Holmes and Dr. Watson are called upon to investigate. The step-father, the local Gypsies, and the furious future mother-in-law are all suspects. And was it really a vampire in the shape of a bat that took the young mother-to-be's life? This adventure takes the world's favorite detective away from London to Surrey, and then north to the lovely but deadly Lake District. The story was inspired by the original Sherlock Holmes story, *The Adventure of the Speckled Band* and like the original, leaves the mind wondering and the heart racing.

The Adventure of the Engineer's Mom.

A brilliant young Cambridge University engineer is carrying out secret research for the Admiralty. It will lead to the building of the world's most powerful battleship, The Dreadnaught. His adventuress mother is kidnapped and having been spurned by Scotland Yard he seeks the help of Sherlock Holmes. Was she taken by German spies, or an underhanded student, or by someone else? Whoever it was is prepared to commit cold-blooded murder to get what they want. Holmes and Watson have help from an unexpected source – the engineer's mom herself. This new mystery is inspired by the original Sherlock Holmes story – *The Engineer's Thumb*.

The Adventure of the Notable Bachelorette.

A snobbish and obnoxious nobleman enters 221B Baker Street demanding the help of Sherlock Holmes in finding his much younger wife – a beautiful and spirited American from the West. Three days later the wife is accused of a vile crime. Now she comes to Sherlock Holmes seeking his help to prove her innocence so she can avoid the gallows. Neither noble husband nor wife have been playing by the rules of Victorian moral behavior. So who did it? The wife? The mistress? The younger brother? Someone unknown? Fans of Sherlock Holmes will enjoy this mystery, set in London during the last years of the nineteenth century, and written in the same voice as the beloved stories of the original canon. This new mystery was inspired by the original Sherlock Holmes story, *The Adventure of the Noble Bachelor.*

The Bald-Headed Trust.

Watson insists on taking Sherlock Holmes on a short vacation to the seaside in Plymouth. No sooner has Holmes arrived than he is needed to solve a double murder and prevent a massive fraud diabolically designed by the evil Professor himself.

Moriarty has found a way to deprive the financial world of millions of pounds without their ever knowing that they have been robbed. Who knew that a family of devout conservative churchgoers could come to the aid of Sherlock Holmes and bring enormous grief to evil doers? The story is inspired by *The Red-Headed League.*

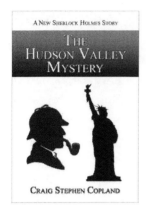

The Hudson Valley Mystery. A young man in New York went mad and murdered his father. Or so say the local police and doctors.

His mother believes he is innocent and knows he is not crazy. She appeals to Sherlock Holmes and, together with Dr. and Mrs. Watson, he crosses the Atlantic to help this client in need. Once there they must duel with the villains of Tammany Hall and with the specter of the legendary headless horseman. This new Sherlock Holmes mystery was inspired by *The Boscombe Valley Mystery*.

The Sign of the Third. Fifteen hundred years ago the courageous Princess Hemamali smuggled the sacred tooth of the Buddha into Ceylon. Since that time it has never left the Temple of the Tooth in Kandy, where it has been guarded and worshiped by the faithful. Now, for the first time, it is being brought to London to be part of a magnificent exhibit at the British Museum. But what if something were to happen to it? It would be a disaster for the British Empire. Sherlock Holmes, Dr. Watson, and even Mycroft Holmes are called upon to prevent such a crisis. Will they prevail? What is about to happen to Dr. John Watson? And who is this mysterious young Irregular they call The Injin? This novella is inspired by the Sherlock Holmes mystery, *The Sign of the Four*.

The Mystery of the Five Oranges.

On a miserable rainy evening, a desperate father enters 221B Baker Street. His daughter has been kidnapped and spirited off the North America. The evil network who have taken her has spies everywhere. If he goes to Scotland Yard, they will kill her. There is only one hope – Sherlock Holmes. Holmes and Watson sail to a small corner of Canada, Prince Edward Island, in search of the girl. They find themselves fighting one of the most powerful and malicious organizations on earth – the Ku Klux Klan. Sherlockians will enjoy this new adventure of the world's most famous detective, inspired by the original story of *The Five Orange Pips*. And those who love *Anne of Green Gab*les will thrill to see her recruited by Holmes and Watson to help in the defeat of crime.

The Adventure of the Blue Belt Buckle

A young street urchin, one of the Baker Street Irregulars, discovers a man's belt and buckle under a bush in Hyde Park. The buckle is unique and stunning, gleaming turquoise stones set in exquisitely carved silver; a masterpiece from the native American west. A body is found in a hotel room in Mayfair. Scotland Yard seeks the help of Sherlock Holmes in solving the murder. The Queen's Diamond Jubilee, to be held in just a few months, could be ruined. Sherlock Holmes, Dr. Watson, Scotland Yard, the Home Office and even Her Majesty all team up to prevent a crime of unspeakable dimensions. A new mystery inspired by *The Blue Carbuncle*.

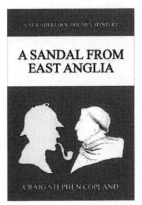

A Sandal from East Anglia.

Archeological excavations at the ruined Abbey of St. Edmund unearth a sealed canister. In it is a document that has the potential to change the course of the British Empire and all of Christendom. There are some evil young men who are prepared to rob, and beat and even commit murder to keep its contents from ever becoming known. There is a strikingly beautiful young Sister, with a curious double life, who is determined to use the document to improve the lives of women throughout the world. The mystery is inspired by the original Sherlock Holmes story, A Scandal in Bohemia. Fans of Sherlock Holmes will enjoy a new story that maintains all the loved and familiar characters and settings of Victorian England.

The Man Who Was Twisted But Hip.

It is 1897 and France is torn apart by The Dreyfus Affair. Westminster needs help from Sherlock Holmes to make sure that the evil tide of anti-Semitism that has engulfed France will not spread. A young officer in the Foreign Office suddenly resigns from his post and enters the theater. His wife calls for help from Sherlock Holmes. The evil professor is up to something, and it could have terrible consequences for the young couple and all of Europe. Sherlock and Watson run all over London and Paris solving the puzzle and seeking to thwart Moriarty. This new mystery is inspired by the original story, *The Man with the Twisted Lip*, as well as by the great classic by Victor Hugo, *The Hunchback of Notre Dame*.

The Adventure of the Coiffured Bitches.

A beautiful young woman will soon inherit a lot of money. She disappears. Her little brother is convinced that she has become a zombie, living and not living in the graveyard of the ruined old church. Another young woman - flirtatious, independent, lovely - agrees to be the nurse to the little brother. She finds out far too much and, in desperation seeks help from Sherlock Holmes, the man she also adores. Sherlock Holmes, Dr. Watson and Miss Violet Hunter must solve the mystery of the coiffured bitches, avoid the massive mastiff that could tear their throats, and protect the boy. The story is inspired by the original Conan Doyle *The Adventure of the Copper Beeches*.

The Adventure of the Beryl Anarchists.

A deeply distressed banker enters 221B Baker St. His safe has been robbed and he is certain that his motorcycle-riding sons have betrayed him. Highly incriminating and embarrassing records of the financial and personal affairs of England's nobility are now in the hands of blackmailers - the Beryl Anarchists - all passionately involved in the craze of motorcycle riding, and in ruthless criminal pursuits. And then a young girl is murdered. Holmes and Watson must find the real culprits and stop them before more crimes are committed - too horrendous to be imagined. This new mystery was inspired by *The Adventure of the Beryl Coronet* and borrows the setting and some of the characters.

The Silver Horse, Braised. The greatest horse race of the century, with the best five-year-olds of England running against the best of America, will take place in a week at Epsom Downs. Millions have been bet on the winners. Owners, jockeys, grooms, and gamblers from across England arrive. So too do a host of colorful characters from the racetracks of America. The race is run and an incredible white horse emerges as the winner by over twenty-five lengths. Celebrations are in order and good times are had. And that night disaster strikes. More deaths, of both men and beasts, take place. Holmes identifies several suspects and then, to his great disappointment and frustration, he fails to prove that any of them committed the crime. Until… This completely original mystery is a tribute to the original Sherlock Holmes story, *Silver Blaze*. It also borrows from the great racetrack stories of Damon Runyon.

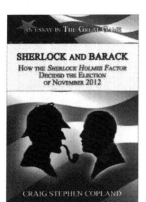

Sherlock and Barack. This is NOT a new Sherlock Holmes Mystery. It is a Sherlockian research paper seeking answers to some very serious questions. Why did Barack Obama win in November 2012? Why did Mitt Romney lose? Pundits and political scientists have offered countless reasons. This book reveals the truth - The Sherlock Holmes Factor. Had it not been for Sherlock Holmes, Mitt Romney would be president. This study is the first entry by Sherlockian Craig Stephen Copland into the Grand Game of amateur analysis of the canon of Sherlock Holmes stories, and their effect on western civilization

The Box of Cards. Two teenagers, a brother and a sister from a strict religious family disappear. The parents are alarmed but Scotland Yard says they are just off sowing their wild oats. A horrific, gruesome package arrives in the post and it becomes clear that a terrible crime is in process. Sherlock Holmes is called in to help. Passions and hatred going back many years are revealed. Holmes, Watson, and Lestrade must act quickly before young lives are lost. This mystery, set in London in 1905, is inspired by the original Sherlock Holmes story, "The Cardboard Box," one of the darkest and most gruesome of the original Canon. If you enjoy the mysteries of Sherlock Holmes, you will again be treated to watching your hero untangle the web of evil and bring justice to all involved.

The Yellow Farce. It is the spring of 1906. Sherlock Holmes is sent by his brother, Mycroft, to Japan. The war between Russia and Japan is raging. Alliances between countries in these years before World War I are fragile and any misstep could plunge the world into Armageddon. The Empire is officially neutral but an American diplomat has been murdered and a British one has disappeared. The wife of the British ambassador is suspected of being a Russian agent. Join Holmes and Watson as they travel around the world to Japan. Once there, they encounter an inscrutable culture, have to solve the mystery, and maybe even save the life of the Emperor. It's a fun read and is inspired by the original Sherlock Holmes story, *The Yellow Face*.

The Three Rhodes Not Taken.

Oxford University is famous throughout the world for its splendid architecture, lovely manicured lawns and gardens, and passionate pursuit of research, teaching and learning. But it turns out to be at the center of a case involving fraud, theft, treachery, and, maybe, murder. The Rhodes Scholarship has been recently established and is seen at one of the greatest prizes available to young men throughout the Empire. So much so that some men are prepared to lie, steal, slander, and, maybe murder, in the pursuit of it. Sherlock Holmes is called upon to track down a thief who has stolen vital documents pertaining to the winner of the scholarship, but what will he do when the prime suspect is found dead? The story was inspired by the original story in the canon, *The Three Students*.

A Most Grave Ritual.

In 1649, King Charles I escaped from the palace in which he was being held prisoner and made a desperate run for Southampton, hoping to reach safety on the Continent. He never made it and was returned to face trial and execution. Did he leave behind a vast fortune that he had taken from the Royal Treasury?

The Musgrave family now owns the old castle where the king may have left his fortune. The patriarch of the family dies in the courtyard and the locals believe that the headless ghost of the king did him in. The police accuse his son of murdering him so he could claim the fortune. Sherlock Holmes is hired to exonerate the lad.

The Stock Market Murders. A young man's friend has gone missing. Holmes and Watson go with him to Birmingham to help look for him. What they find is horrifying. Two more bodies of young men turn up in London. All of the victims are tied to Cambridge University. All are also tied to the financial sector of the City and to one of the greatest frauds ever visited upon the citizens of England. The story is based on the true story of James Whitaker Wright and is inspired by the original Sherlock Holmes story, The Stock Broker's Clerk. Any resemblance of the villain to a certain presidential candidate is entirely coincidental.

Reverend Ezekiel Black—'The Sherlock Holmes of the American West'—Mystery Stories.

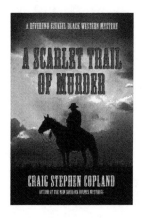

A Scarlet Trail of Murder. At ten o'clock on Sunday morning, the twenty-second of October, 1882, in an abandoned house in the West Bottom of Kansas City, a fellow named Jasper Harrison did not wake up. His inability to do was the result of his having had his throat cut sometime during the previous night. At the same time, in the same location, Eddie Kepler did wake up. Eddie staggered out into the blinding daylight and started hollering very loudly for the police. I know these things because by noon on that same day, I was kneeling down on the floor beside my new partner, the Reverend Mister Ezekiel Amos Black, and together we were examining the body of Mr. Jasper Harrison. Three weeks and nearly three thousand miles later, the Rev had not only brought the murderer to justice but had helped solve several other murders and some very nasty deeds that stretched back over fifteen years. This story of mine, written so as to be appropriate to all members of your family, about the brainiest and downright strangest preacher and part-time Deputy US Marshal, is going to tell you how that all came about. And I am not going to be at all surprised if, after reading it, you will agree with me that Reverend Ezekiel Black was certainly one very smart man but, my goodness, was he a strange bird.   Jim Watson, MD

This original western mystery was inspired by The great Sherlock Holmes classic, *A Study in Scarlet*.

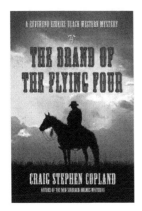

The Brand of the Flying Four. This case all began one quiet evening—very quiet; bordering on boring—while we were sitting by the hearth in our rooms in Kansas City. A few weeks later, a murder, perhaps the most gruesome I had ever witnessed in all my born days, took place in Denver, immediately above our heads. By the time it all ended, justice, of the frontier variety, not the courtroom, had been meted out. If you want to know how it all happened, you'll have to read this story. Jim Watson, M.D. Denver, 1883

The story is inspired by *The Sign of the Four"* by Arthur Conan Doyle, and like that story it combines murder most foul, and romance most enticing.

Collection Sets for ebooks– each with several more new Sherlock Holmes mysteries – are available as boxed sets at *40% off the price of buying them separately.*

Collection One

The Sign of the Third

The Hudson Valley Mystery

A Case of Identity Theft

The Bald-Headed Trust

Studying Scarlet

The Mystery of the Five Oranges

Collection Two

A Sandal from East Anglia

The Man Who Was Twisted But Hip

The Blue Belt Buckle

The Spectred Bat

Collection Three

The Engineer's Mom

The Notable Bachelorette

The Beryl Anarchists

The Coiffured Bitches

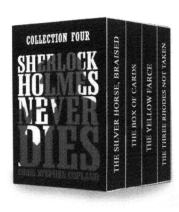

Collection Four

The Silver Horse, Braised

The Box of Cards

The Yellow Farce

The Three Rhodes Not Taken

As our way of thanking you for purchasing this book, you can now download six more new Sherlock Holmes mysteries for free.

Go now to

www.SherlockHolmesMystery.com, subscribe to Craig Stephen Copland's Irregular Newsletter, get six new mysteries **FREE**, and start enjoying more Sherlock now.

The Gloria Scott

The Original Sherlock Holmes Story

Arthur Conan Doyle

The Gloria Scott

"I have some papers here," said my friend Sherlock Holmes, as we sat one winter's night on either side of the fire, "which I really think, Watson, that it would be worth your while to glance over. These are the documents in the extraordinary case of the Gloria Scott, and this is the message which struck Justice of the Peace Trevor dead with horror when he read it."

He had picked from a drawer a little tarnished cylinder, and, undoing the tape, he handed me a short note scrawled upon a half-sheet of slate-gray paper.

"The supply of game for London is going steadily up," it ran. "Head-keeper Hudson, we believe, has been now told to receive all orders for fly-paper and for preservation of your hen-pheasant's life."

As I glanced up from reading this enigmatical message, I saw Holmes chuckling at the expression upon my face.

"You look a little bewildered," said he.

"I cannot see how such a message as this could inspire horror. It seems to me to be rather grotesque than otherwise."

"Very likely. Yet the fact remains that the reader, who was a fine, robust old man, was knocked clean down by it as if it had been the butt end of a pistol."

"You arouse my curiosity," said I. "But why did you say just now that there were very particular reasons why I should study this case?"

"Because it was the first in which I was ever engaged."

I had often endeavored to elicit from my companion what had first turned his mind in the direction of criminal research, but had never caught him before in a communicative humor. Now he sat forward in this arm-chair and spread out the documents upon his knees. Then he lit his pipe and sat for some time smoking and turning them over.

"You never heard me talk of Victor Trevor?" he asked. "He was the only friend I made during the two years I was at college. I was never a very sociable fellow, Watson, always rather fond of moping in my rooms and working out my own little methods of thought, so that I never mixed much with the men of my year. Bar fencing and boxing I had few athletic tastes, and then my line of study was quite distinct from that of the other fellows, so that we had no points of contact at all. Trevor was the only man I knew, and that only through the accident of his bull terrier freezing on to my ankle one morning as I went down to chapel.

"It was a prosaic way of forming a friendship, but it was effective. I was laid by the heels for ten days, but Trevor used to come in to inquire after me. At first it was only a minute's chat, but soon his visits lengthened, and before the end of the term we were close friends. He was a hearty, full-blooded fellow, full of spirits and energy, the very opposite to me in most respects, but we had some subjects in common, and it was a bond of union when I found that he was as friendless as I. Finally, he invited me down to his father's place at Donnithorpe, in Norfolk, and I accepted his hospitality for a month of the long vacation.

"Old Trevor was evidently a man of some wealth and consideration, a J.P., and a landed proprietor. Donnithorpe is a little hamlet just to the north of Langmere, in the country of the Broads. The house was an old-fashioned, wide-spread, oak-beamed brick building, with a fine lime-lined avenue leading up to it. There was excellent wild-duck shooting in the fens, remarkably good fishing, a small but select library, taken over, as I understood, from a former occupant, and a tolerable cook, so that he would be a fastidious man who could not put in a pleasant month there.

"Trevor senior was a widower, and my friend his only son.

"There had been a daughter, I heard, but she had died of diphtheria while on a visit to Birmingham. The father interested me extremely. He was a man of little culture, but with a considerable amount of rude strength, both physically and mentally. He knew hardly any books, but he had traveled far, had seen much of the world. And had remembered all that he had learned. In person he was a thick-set, burly man with a shock of grizzled hair, a brown, weather-beaten face, and blue eyes which were keen to the verge of fierceness. Yet he had a reputation for kindness and charity on the country-side, and was noted for the leniency of his sentences from the bench.

"One evening, shortly after my arrival, we were sitting over a glass of port after dinner, when young Trevor began to talk about those habits of observation and inference which I had already formed into a system, although I had not yet appreciated the part which they were to play in my life. The old man evidently thought that his son was exaggerating in his description of one or two trivial feats which I had performed.

"'Come, now, Mr. Holmes,' said he, laughing good-humoredly. 'I'm an excellent subject, if you can deduce anything from me.'

"'I fear there is not very much,' I answered; 'I might suggest that you have gone about in fear of some personal attack within the last twelvemonth.'

"The laugh faded from his lips, and he stared at me in great surprise.

"'Well, that's true enough,' said he. 'You know, Victor,' turning to his son, 'when we broke up that poaching gang they swore to knife us, and Sir Edward Holly has actually been attacked. I've always been on my guard since then, though I have no idea how you know it.'

"'You have a very handsome stick,' I answered. 'By the inscription I observed that you had not had it more than a year. But you have taken some pains to bore the head of it and pour melted lead into the hole so as to make it a formidable weapon. I argued that you would not take such precautions unless you had some danger to fear.'

"'Anything else?' he asked, smiling.

"'You have boxed a good deal in your youth.'

"'Right again. How did you know it? Is my nose knocked a little out of the straight?'

"'No,' said I. 'It is your ears. They have the peculiar flattening and thickening which marks the boxing man.'

"'Anything else?'

"'You have done a good deal of digging by your callosities.'

"'Made all my money at the gold fields.'

"'You have been in New Zealand.'

"'Right again.'

"'You have visited Japan.'

"'Quite true.'

"'And you have been most intimately associated with some one whose initials were J. A., and whom you afterwards were eager to entirely forget.'

"Mr. Trevor stood slowly up, fixed his large blue eyes upon me with a strange wild stare, and then pitched forward, with his face among the nutshells which strewed the cloth, in a dead faint.

"You can imagine, Watson, how shocked both his son and I were. His attack did not last long, however, for when we undid his collar, and sprinkled the water from one of the finger-glasses over his face, he gave a gasp or two and sat up.

"'Ah, boys,' said he, forcing a smile, 'I hope I haven't frightened you. Strong as I look, there is a weak place in my heart, and it does not take much to knock me over. I don't know how you manage this, Mr. Holmes, but it seems to me that all the detectives of fact and of fancy would be children in your hands. That's your line of life, sir, and you may take the word of a man who has seen something of the world.'

"And that recommendation, with the exaggerated estimate of my ability with which he prefaced it, was, if you will believe me, Watson, the very first thing which ever made me feel that a profession might be made out of what had up to that time been the merest hobby. At the moment, however, I was too much concerned at the sudden illness of my host to think of anything else.

"'I hope that I have said nothing to pain you?' said I.

"'Well, you certainly touched upon rather a tender point. Might I ask how you know, and how much you know?' He spoke now in a half-jesting fashion, but a look of terror still lurked at the back of his eyes.

"'It is simplicity itself,' said I. 'When you bared your arm to draw that fish into the boat I saw that J. A., had been tattooed in the bend of the elbow. The letters were still legible, but it was perfectly clear from their blurred appearance, and from the staining of the skin round them, that efforts had been made to obliterate them. It was obvious, then, that those initials had once been very familiar to you, and that you had afterwards wished to forget them.'

"What an eye you have!" he cried, with a sigh of relief. 'It is just as you say. But we won't talk of it. Of all ghosts the ghosts of our old lovers are the worst. Come into the billiard-room and have a quiet cigar.'

"From that day, amid all his cordiality, there was always a touch of suspicion in Mr. Trevor's manner towards me. Even his son remarked it. 'You've given the governor such a turn,' said he, 'that he'll never be sure again of what you know and what you don't know.' He did not mean to show it, I am sure, but it was so strongly in his mind that it peeped out at every action. At last I became so convinced that I was causing him uneasiness that I drew my visit to a close. On the very day, however, before I left, an incident occurred which proved in the sequel to be of importance.

"We were sitting out upon the lawn on garden chairs, the three of us, basking in the sun and admiring the view across the Broads, when a maid came out to say that there was a man at the door who wanted to see Mr. Trevor.

"'What is his name?' asked my host.

"'He would not give any.'

"'What does he want, then?'

"'He says that you know him, and that he only wants a moment's conversation.'

"'Show him round here.' An instant afterwards there appeared a little wizened fellow with a cringing manner and a shambling style of walking. He wore an open jacket, with a splotch of tar on the sleeve, a red-and-black check shirt, dungaree trousers, and heavy boots badly worn. His face was thin and brown and crafty, with a perpetual smile upon it, which showed an irregular line of yellow teeth, and his crinkled hands were half closed in a way that is distinctive of sailors. As he came slouching across the lawn I heard Mr. Trevor make a sort of hiccoughing noise in his throat, and jumping out of his chair, he ran into the house. He was back in a moment, and I smelt a strong reek of brandy as he passed me.

"'Well, my man,' said he. 'What can I do for you?'

"The sailor stood looking at him with puckered eyes, and with the same loose-lipped smile upon his face.

"'You don't know me?' he asked.

"'Why, dear me, it is surely Hudson,' said Mr. Trevor in a tone of surprise.

"'Hudson it is, sir,' said the seaman. 'Why, it's thirty year and more since I saw you last. Here you are in your house, and me still picking my salt meat out of the harness cask.'

"'Tut, you will find that I have not forgotten old times,' cried Mr. Trevor, and, walking towards the sailor, he said something in a low voice. 'Go into the kitchen,' he continued out loud, 'and you will get food and drink. I have no doubt that I shall find you a situation.'

"'Thank you, sir,' said the seaman, touching his fore-lock. 'I'm just off a two-yearer in an eight-knot tramp, short-handed at that, and I wants a rest. I thought I'd get it either with Mr. Beddoes or with you.'

"'Ah!' cried Trevor. 'You know where Mr. Beddoes is?'

"'Bless you, sir, I know where all my old friends are,' said the fellow with a sinister smile, and he slouched off after the maid to the kitchen. Mr. Trevor mumbled something to us about having been shipmate with the man when he was going back to the diggings, and then, leaving us on the lawn, he went indoors. An hour later, when we entered the house, we found him stretched dead drunk upon the dining-room sofa. The whole incident left a most ugly impression upon my mind, and I was not sorry next day to leave Donnithorpe behind me, for I felt that my presence must be a source of embarrassment to my friend.

"All this occurred during the first month of the long vacation. I went up to my London rooms, where I spent seven weeks working out a few experiments in organic chemistry. One day, however, when the autumn was far advanced and the vacation drawing to a close, I received a telegram from my friend imploring me to return to Donnithorpe, and saying that he was in great need of my advice and assistance. Of course I dropped everything and set out for the North once more.

"He met me with the dog-cart at the station, and I saw at a

glance that the last two months had been very trying ones for him. He had grown thin and careworn, and had lost the loud, cheery manner for which he had been remarkable.

"'The governor is dying,' were the first words he said.

"'Impossible!' I cried. 'What is the matter?'

"'Apoplexy. Nervous shock, He's been on the verge all day. I doubt if we shall find him alive.'

"I was, as you may think, Watson, horrified at this unexpected news.

"'What has caused it?' I asked.

"'Ah, that is the point. Jump in and we can talk it over while we drive. You remember that fellow who came upon the evening before you left us?'

"'Perfectly.'

"'Do you know who it was that we let into the house that day?'

"'I have no idea.'

"'It was the devil, Holmes,' he cried.

"I stared at him in astonishment.

"'Yes, it was the devil himself. We have not had a peaceful hour since—not one. The governor has never held up his head from that evening, and now the life has been crushed out of him and his heart broken, all through this accursed Hudson.'

"'What power had he, then?'

"'Ah, that is what I would give so much to know. The kindly, charitable, good old governor—how could he have fallen into the clutches of such a ruffian! But I am so glad that you have come, Holmes. I trust very much to your judgment and discretion, and I know that you will advise me for the best.'

"We were dashing along the smooth white country road, with the long stretch of the Broads in front of us glimmering in the red light of the setting sun. From a grove upon our left I could already see the high chimneys and the flag-staff which marked the squire's dwelling.

"'My father made the fellow gardener,' said my companion, 'and then, as that did not satisfy him, he was promoted to be butler. The house seemed to be at his mercy, and he wandered about and did what he chose in it. The maids complained of his drunken habits and his vile language. The dad raised their wages all round to recompense them for the annoyance. The fellow would take the boat and my father's best gun and treat himself to little shooting trips. And all this with such a sneering, leering, insolent face that I would have knocked him down twenty times over if he had been a man of my own age. I tell you, Holmes, I have had to keep a tight hold upon myself all this time; and now I am asking myself whether, if I had let myself go a little more, I might not have been a wiser man.

"'Well, matters went from bad to worse with us, and this animal Hudson became more and more intrusive, until at last, on making some insolent reply to my father in my presence one day, I took him by the shoulders and turned him out of the room. He slunk away with a livid face and two venomous eyes which uttered more threats than his tongue could do. I don't know what passed between the poor dad and him after that, but the dad came to me next day and asked me whether I would mind apologizing to Hudson. I refused, as you can imagine, and asked my father how he could allow such a wretch to take such liberties with himself and his household.

"Ah, my boy," said he, "it is all very well to talk, but you don't know how I am placed. But you shall know, Victor. I'll see that you shall know, come what may. You wouldn't believe harm of your poor old father, would you, lad?" He was very much moved, and shut himself up in the study all day, where I could see through the window that he was writing busily.

"'That evening there came what seemed to me to be a grand release, for Hudson told us that he was going to leave us. He walked into the dining-room as we sat after dinner, and announced his intention in the thick voice of a half-drunken man.

"I've had enough of Norfolk," said he. "I'll run down to Mr. Beddoes in Hampshire. He'll be as glad to see me as you were, I dare say."

"You're not going away in an unkind spirit, Hudson, I hope," said my father, with a tameness which made my blood boil.

"I've not had my 'pology," said he sulkily, glancing in my direction.

"Victor, you will acknowledge that you have used this worthy fellow rather roughly," said the dad, turning to me.

"On the contrary, I think that we have both shown extraordinary patience towards him," I answered.

"Oh, you do, do you?" he snarls. "Very good, mate. We'll see about that!"

"'He slouched out of the room, and half an hour afterwards left the house, leaving my father in a state of pitiable nervousness. Night after night I heard him pacing his room, and it was just as he was recovering his confidence that the blow did at last fall.'

"'And how?' I asked eagerly.

"'In a most extraordinary fashion. A letter arrived for my father yesterday evening, bearing the Fordingbridge post-mark. My father read it, clapped both his hands to his head, and began running round the room in little circles like a man who has been driven out of his senses. When I at last drew him down on to the sofa, his mouth and eyelids were all puckered on one side, and I saw that he had a stroke. Dr. Fordham came over at once. We put him to bed; but the paralysis has spread, he has shown no sign of returning consciousness, and I think that we shall hardly find him alive.'

"'You horrify me, Trevor!' I cried. 'What then could have been in this letter to cause so dreadful a result?'

"'Nothing. There lies the inexplicable part of it. The message was absurd and trivial. Ah, my God, it is as I feared!'

"As he spoke we came round the curve of the avenue, and saw in the fading light that every blind in the house had been drawn down. As we dashed up to the door, my friend's face convulsed with grief, a gentleman in black emerged from it.

"'When did it happen, doctor?' asked Trevor.

"'Almost immediately after you left.'

"'Did he recover consciousness?'

"'For an instant before the end.'

"'Any message for me.'

"'Only that the papers were in the back drawer of the Japanese cabinet.'
a ship

"My friend ascended with the doctor to the chamber of death, while I remained in the study, turning the whole matter over and over in my head, and feeling as sombre as ever I had done in my life. What was the past of this Trevor, pugilist, traveler, and gold-digger, and how had he placed himself in the power of this acid-faced seaman? Why, too, should he faint at an allusion to the half-effaced initials upon his arm, and die of fright when he had a letter from Fordingham? Then I remembered that Fordingham was in Hampshire, and that this Mr. Beddoes, whom the seaman had gone to visit and presumably to blackmail, had also been mentioned as living in Hampshire. The letter, then, might either come from Hudson, the seaman, saying that he had betrayed the guilty secret which appeared to exist, or it might come from Beddoes, warning an old confederate that such a betrayal was imminent. So far it seemed clear enough. But then how could this letter be trivial and grotesque, as describe by the son? He must have misread it. If so, it must have been one of those ingenious secret codes which mean one thing while they seem to mean another. I must see this letter. If there were a hidden meaning in it, I was confident that I could pluck it forth.

109

For an hour I sat pondering over it in the gloom, until at last a weeping maid brought in a lamp, and close at her heels came my friend Trevor, pale but composed, with these very papers which lie upon my knee held in his grasp. He sat down opposite to me, drew the lamp to the edge of the table, and handed me a short note scribbled, as you see, upon a single sheet of gray paper. 'The supply of game for London is going steadily up,' it ran. 'Head-keeper Hudson, we believe, has been now told to receive all orders for fly-paper and for preservation of your hen-pheasant's life.'

"I dare say my face looked as bewildered as yours did just now when first I read this message. Then I reread it very carefully. It was evidently as I had thought, and some secret meaning must lie buried in this strange combination of words. Or could it be that there was a prearranged significance to such phrases as 'fly-paper' and 'hen-pheasant'? Such a meaning would be arbitrary and could not be deduced in any way. And yet I was loath to believe that this was the case, and the presence of the word Hudson seemed to show that the subject of the message was as I had guessed, and that it was from Beddoes rather than the sailor. I tried it backwards, but the combination 'life pheasant's hen' was not encouraging. Then I tried alternate words, but neither 'the of for' nor 'supply game London' promised to throw any light upon it.

"And then in an instant the key of the riddle was in my hands, and I saw that every third word, beginning with the first, would give a message which might well drive old Trevor to despair.

"It was short and terse, the warning, as I now read it to my companion:

"'The game is up. Hudson has told all. Fly for your life.'

"Victor Trevor sank his face into his shaking hands, 'It must be that, I suppose,' said he. "This is worse than death, for it means disgrace as well. But what is the meaning of these "head-keepers" and "hen-pheasants"?'

"'It means nothing to the message, but it might mean a good

deal to us if we had no other means of discovering the sender. You see that he has begun by writing "The...game...is," and so on. Afterwards he had, to fulfill the prearranged cipher, to fill in any two words in each space. He would naturally use the first words which came to his mind, and if there were so many which referred to sport among them, you may be tolerably sure that he is either an ardent shot or interested in breeding. Do you know anything of this Beddoes?'

"'Why, now that you mention it,' said he, 'I remember that my poor father used to have an invitation from him to shoot over his preserves every autumn.'

"'Then it is undoubtedly from him that the note comes,' said I. 'It only remains for us to find out what this secret was which the sailor Hudson seems to have held over the heads of these two wealthy and respected men.'

"'Alas, Holmes, I fear that it is one of sin and shame!' cried my friend. 'But from you I shall have no secrets. Here is the statement which was drawn up by my father when he knew that the danger from Hudson had become imminent. I found it in the Japanese cabinet, as he told the doctor. Take it and read it to me, for I have neither the strength nor the courage to do it myself.'

"These are the very papers, Watson, which he handed to me, and I will read them to you, as I read them in the old study that night to him. They are endorsed outside, as you see, 'Some particulars of the voyage of the bark Gloria Scott , from her leaving Falmouth on the 8th October, 1855, to her destruction in N. Lat. 15 degrees 20', W. Long. 25 degrees 14' on Nov. 6th.' It is in the form of a letter, and runs in this way:

"'My dear, dear son, now that approaching disgrace begins to darken the closing years of my life, I can write with all truth and honesty that it is not the terror of the law, it is not the loss of my position in the county, nor is it my fall in the eyes of all who have known me, which cuts me to the heart; but it is the thought that you should come to blush for me—you who love me and who have seldom, I hope, had reason to do other than respect me. But if the blow falls which is forever hanging over me, then I should wish you to read this, that you may know straight from me how far I have been to blame. On the other hand, if all should go well (which may kind God Almighty grant!), then if by any chance this paper should be still undestroyed and should fall into your hands, I conjure you, by all you hold sacred, by the memory of your dear mother, and by the love which had been between us, to hurl it into the fire and to never give one thought to it again.

"'If then your eye goes on to read this line, I know that I shall already have been exposed and dragged from my home, or as is more likely, for you know that my heart is weak, by lying with my tongue sealed forever in death. In either case the time for suppression is past, and every word which I tell you is the naked truth, and this I swear as I hope for mercy.

"'My name, dear lad, is not Trevor. I was James Armitage in my younger days, and you can understand now the shock that it was to me a few weeks ago when your college friend addressed me in words which seemed to imply that he had surprised my secret. As Armitage it was that I entered a London banking-house, and as Armitage I was convicted of breaking my country's laws, and was sentenced to transportation. Do not think very harshly of me, laddie. It was a debt of honor, so called, which I had to pay, and I used money which was not my own to do it, in the certainty that I could replace it before there could be any possibility of its being missed. But the most dreadful ill-luck pursued me. The money which I had reckoned upon never came to hand, and a premature examination of accounts exposed my deficit. The case might have been dealt leniently with, but the laws were more harshly administered thirty years ago than now, and on my twenty-third birthday I found myself chained as a felon with thirty-seven other convicts in 'tween-decks of the bark Gloria Scott , bound for Australia.

"'It was the year '55 when the Crimean war was at its height, and the old convict ships had been largely used as transports in the Black Sea. The government was compelled, therefore, to use smaller and less suitable vessels for sending out their prisoners. The Gloria Scott had been in the Chinese tea-trade, but she was an old-fashioned, heavy-bowed, broad-beamed craft, and the new clippers had cut her out. She was a five-hundred-ton boat; and besides her thirty-eight jail-birds, she carried twenty-six of a crew, eighteen soldiers, a captain, three mates, a doctor, a chaplain, and four warders. Nearly a hundred souls were in her, all told, when we set sail from Falmouth.

"'The partitions between the cells of the convicts, instead of being of thick oak, as is usual in convict-ships, were quite thin and frail. The man next to me, upon the aft side, was one whom I had particularly noticed when we were led down the quay. He was a young man with a clear, hairless face, a long, thin nose, and rather nut-cracker jaws. He carried his head very jauntily in the air, had a swaggering style of walking, and was, above all else, remarkable for his extraordinary height. I don't think any of our heads would have come up to his shoulder, and I am sure that he could not have measured less than six and a half feet. It was strange among so many sad and weary faces to see one which was full of energy and resolution. The sight of it was to me like a fire in a snow-storm. I was glad, then, to find that he was my neighbor, and gladder still when, in the dead of the night, I heard a whisper close to my ear, and found that he had managed to cut an opening in the board which separated us.

"Hullo, chummy!" said he, "what's your name, and what are you here for?"

"'I answered him, and asked in turn who I was talking with.

"I'm Jack Prendergast," said he, "and by God! You'll learn to bless my name before you've done with me."

"'I remembered hearing of his case, for it was one which had made an immense sensation throughout the country some time before my own arrest. He was a man of good family and of great ability, but of incurably vicious habits, who had by an ingenious system of fraud obtained huge sums of money from the leading London merchants.

"Ha, ha! You remember my case!" said he proudly.

"Very well, indeed."

"Then maybe you remember something queer about it?"

"What was that, then?"

"I'd had nearly a quarter of a million, hadn't I?"

"So it was said."

"But none was recovered, eh?"

"No."

"Well, where d'ye suppose the balance is?" he asked.

"I have no idea," said I.

"Right between my finger and thumb," he cried. "By God! I've got more pounds to my name than you've hairs on your head. And if you've money, my son, and know how to handle it and spread it, you can do anything. Now, you don't think it likely that a man who could do anything is going to wear his breeches out sitting in the stinking hold of a rat-gutted, beetle-ridden, mouldy old coffin of a Chin China coaster. No, sir, such a man will look after himself and will look after his chums. You may lay to that! You hold on to him, and you may kiss the book that he'll haul you through."

"'That was his style of talk, and at first I thought it meant nothing; but after a while, when he had tested me and sworn me in with all possible solemnity, he let me understand that there really was a plot to gain command of the vessel. A dozen of the prisoners had hatched it before they came aboard, Prendergast was the leader, and his money was the motive power.

"I'd a partner," said he, "a rare good man, as true as a stock to a barrel. He's got the dibbs, he has, and where do you think he is at this moment? Why, he's the chaplain of this ship—the chaplain, no less! He came aboard with a black coat, and his papers right, and money enough in his box to buy the thing right up from keel to main-truck. The crew are his, body and soul. He could buy 'em at so much a gross with a cash discount, and he did it before ever they signed on. He's got two of the warders and Mereer, the second mate, and he'd get the captain himself, if he thought him worth it."

"What are we to do, then?" I asked.

"What do you think?" said he. "We'll make the coats of some of these soldiers redder than ever the tailor did."

"But they are armed," said I.

"And so shall we be, my boy. There's a brace of pistols for every mother's son of us, and if we can't carry this ship, with the crew at our back, it's time we were all sent to a young misses' boarding-school. You speak to your mate upon the left to-night, and see if he is to be trusted."

"'I did so, and found my other neighbor to be a young fellow in much the same position as myself, whose crime had been forgery. His name was Evans, but he afterwards changed it, like myself, and he is now a rich and prosperous man in the south of England. He was ready enough to join the conspiracy, as the only means of saving ourselves, and before we had crossed the Bay there were only two of the prisoners who were not in the secret. One of these was of weak mind, and we did not dare to trust him, and the other was suffering from jaundice, and could not be of any use to us.

"'From the beginning there was really nothing to prevent us from taking possession of the ship. The crew were a set of ruffians, specially picked for the job. The sham chaplain came into our cells to exhort us, carrying a black bag, supposed to be full of tracts, and so often did he come that by the third day we had each stowed away at the foot of our beds a file, a brace of pistols, a pound of powder, and twenty slugs. Two of the warders were agents of Prendergast, and the second mate was his right-hand man. The captain, the two mates, two warders Lieutenant Martin, his eighteen soldiers, and the doctor were all that we had against us. Yet, safe as it was, we determined to neglect no precaution, and to make our attack suddenly by night. It came, however, more quickly than we expected, and in this way.

"'One evening, about the third week after our start, the doctor had come down to see one of the prisoners who was ill, and putting his hand down on the bottom of his bunk he felt the outline of the pistols. If he had been silent he might have blown the whole thing, but he was a nervous little chap, so he gave a cry of surprise and turned so pale that the man knew what was up in an instant and seized him. He was gagged before he could give the alarm, and tied down upon the bed. He had unlocked the door that led to the deck, and we were through it in a rush. The two sentries were shot down, and so was a corporal who came running to see what was the matter. There were two more soldiers at the door of the state-room, and their muskets seemed not to be loaded, for they never fired upon us, and they were shot while trying to fix their bayonets. Then we rushed on into the captain's cabin, but as we pushed open the door there was an explosion from within, and there he lay with his brains smeared over the chart of the Atlantic which was pinned upon the table, while the chaplain stood with a smoking pistol in his hand at his elbow. The two mates had both been seized by the crew, and the whole business seemed to be settled.

"'The state-room was next the cabin, and we flocked in there and flopped down on the settees, all speaking together, for we were just mad with the feeling that we were free once more. There were lockers all round, and Wilson, the sham chaplain, knocked one of them in, and pulled out a dozen of brown sherry. We cracked off the necks of the bottles, poured the stuff out into tumblers, and were just tossing them off, when in an instant without warning there came the roar of muskets in our ears, and the saloon was so full of smoke that we could not see across the table. When it cleared again the place was a shambles. Wilson and eight others were wriggling on the top of each other on the floor, and the blood and the brown sherry on that table turn me sick now when I think of it. We were so cowed by the sight that I think we should have given the job up if it had not been for Prendergast. He bellowed like a bull and rushed for the door with all that were left alive at his heels. Out we ran, and there on the poop were the lieutenant and ten of his men. The swing skylights above the saloon table had been a bit open, and they had fired on us through the slit. We got on them before they could load, and they stood to it like men; but we had the upper hand of them, and in five minutes it was all over. My God! Was there ever a slaughter-house like that ship! Prendergast was like a raging devil, and he picked the soldiers up as if they had been children and threw them overboard alive or dead. There was one sergeant that was horribly wounded and yet kept on swimming for a surprising time, until some one in mercy blew out his brains. When the fighting was over there was no one left of our enemies except just the warders the mates, and the doctor.

"'It was over them that the great quarrel arose. There were many of us who were glad enough to win back our freedom, and yet who had no wish to have murder on our souls. It was one thing to knock the soldiers over with their muskets in their hands, and it was another to stand by while men were being killed in cold blood. Eight of us, five convicts and three sailors, said that we would not see it done. But there was no moving Prendergast and those who were with him. Our only chance of safety lay in making a clean job of it, said he, and he would not leave a tongue with power to wag in a witness-box. It nearly came to our sharing the fate of the prisoners, but at last he said that if we wished we might take a boat and go. We jumped at the offer, for we were already sick of these bloodthirsty doings, and we saw that there would be worse before it was done. We were given a suit of sailor togs each, a barrel of water, two casks, one of junk and one of biscuits, and a compass. Prendergast threw us over a chart, told us that we were shipwrecked mariners whose ship had foundered in Lat. 15 degrees and Long 25 degrees west, and then cut the painter and let us go.

"'And now I come to the most surprising part of my story, my dear son. The seamen had hauled the fore-yard aback during the rising, but now as we left them they brought it square again, and as there was a light wind from the north and east the bark began to draw slowly away from us. Our boat lay, rising and falling, upon the long, smooth rollers, and Evans and I, who were the most educated of the party, were sitting in the sheets working out our position and planning what coast we should make for. It was a nice question, for the Cape de Verdes were about five hundred miles to the north of us, and the African coast about seven hundred to the east. On the whole, as the wind was coming round to the north, we thought that Sierra Leone might be best, and turned our head in that direction, the bark being at that time nearly hull down on our starboard quarter. Suddenly as we looked at her we saw a dense black cloud of smoke shoot up from her, which hung like a monstrous tree upon the sky line. A few seconds later a roar like thunder burst upon our ears, and as the smoke thinned away there was no sign left of the Gloria Scott . In an instant we swept the boat's head round again and pulled with all our strength for the place where the haze still trailing over the water marked the scene of this catastrophe.

"'It was a long hour before we reached it, and at first we feared that we had come too late to save any one. A splintered boat and a number of crates and fragments of spars rising and falling on the waves showed us where the vessel had foundered; but there was no sign of life, and we had turned away in despair when we heard a cry for help, and saw at some distance a piece of wreckage with a man lying stretched across it. When we pulled him aboard the boat he proved to be a young seaman of the name of Hudson, who was so burned and exhausted that he could give us no account of what had happened until the following morning.

"'It seemed that after we had left, Prendergast and his gang had proceeded to put to death the five remaining prisoners. The two warders had been shot and thrown overboard, and so also had the third mate. Prendergast then descended into the 'tween-decks and with his own hands cut the throat of the unfortunate surgeon. There only remained the first mate, who was a bold and active man. When he saw the convict approaching him with the bloody knife in his hand he kicked off his bonds, which he had somehow contrived to loosen, and rushing down the deck he plunged into the after-hold. A dozen convicts, who descended with their pistols in search of him, found him with a match-box in his hand seated beside an open powder-barrel, which was one of a hundred carried on board, and swearing that he would blow all hands up if he were in any way molested. An instant later the explosion occurred, though Hudson thought it was caused by the misdirected bullet of one of the convicts rather than the mate's match. Be the cause what it may, it was the end of the Gloria Scott and of the rabble who held command of her.

"'Such, in a few words, my dear boy, is the history of this terrible business in which I was involved. Next day we were picked up by the brig Hotspur , bound for Australia, whose captain found no difficulty in believing that we were the survivors of a passenger ship which had foundered. The transport ship Gloria Scott was set down by the Admiralty as being lost at sea, and no word has ever leaked out as to her true fate. After an excellent voyage the Hotspur landed us at Sydney, where Evans and I changed our names and made our way to the diggings, where, among the crowds who were gathered from all nations, we had no difficulty in losing our former identities. The rest I need not relate. We prospered, we traveled, we came back as rich colonials to England, and we bought country estates. For more than twenty years we have led peaceful and useful lives, and we hoped that our past was forever buried. Imagine, then, my feelings when in the seaman who came to us I recognized instantly the man who had been picked off the wreck. He had tracked us down somehow, and had set himself to live upon our fears. You will understand now how it was that I strove to keep the peace with him, and you will in some measure sympathize with me in the fears which fill me, now that he has gone from me to his other victim with threats upon his tongue.'

"Underneath is written in a hand so shaky as to be hardly legible, 'Beddoes writes in cipher to say H., has told all. Sweet Lord, have mercy on our souls!'

"That was the narrative which I read that night to young Trevor, and I think, Watson, that under the circumstances it was a dramatic one. The good fellow was heart-broken at it, and went out to the Terai tea planting, where I hear that he is doing well. As to the sailor and Beddoes, neither of them was ever heard of again after that day on which the letter of warning was written. They both disappeared utterly and completely. No complaint had been lodged with the police, so that Beddoes had mistaken a threat for a deed. Hudson had been seen lurking about, and it was believed by the police that he had done away with Beddoes and had fled. For myself I believe that the truth was exactly the opposite. I think that it is most probable that Beddoes, pushed to desperation and believing himself to have been already betrayed, had revenged himself upon Hudson, and had fled from the country with as much money as he could lay his hands on. Those are the facts of the case, Doctor, and if they are of any use to your collection, I am sure that they are very heartily at your service."

Made in the USA
San Bernardino, CA
14 January 2017